HERMAN

László Krasznahorkai

HERMAN

The Game Warden &
The Death of a Craft

Translated from the Hungarian
by John Batki

A NEW DIRECTIONS BOOK

Manufactured in the United States of America
New Directions Books are printed on acid-free paper
First published as a New Directions Book in 2016
Design by Erik Rieselbach

Library of Congress Cataloging-in-Publication Data
Names: Krasznahorkai, László, author. | Szirtes, George, 1948– translator. |
Batki, John, translator. | Krasznahorkai, László. Utolsó farkas. English. |
Krasznahorkai, László. Herman, a vadőr. English. Title: The last wolf ;
& Herman : the game warden, the death of a craft / Laszlo Krasznahorkai ;
translated from the Hungarian by George Szirtes and John Batki.
Other titles: The last wolf and Herman
Description: New York : New Directions Publishing Corporation, 2016. |
"Originally published in Hungarian as Az utolsó farkas (The Last Wolf,
originally published 2009), and Herman, a vadőr, A mesterségnek vége
(Herman, originally published 1986)"—Title page verso.
Identifiers: LCCN 2016022374 (print) | LCCN 2016035509 (ebook) |
ISBN 9780811226080 (alk. paper) | ISBN 9780811226097 ()
Classification: LCC PH3281.K8866 A2 2016 (print) |
LCC PH3281.K8866 (ebook) | DDC 894/.51134—dc23
LC record available at https://lccn.loc.gov/2016022374

2 4 6 8 10 9 7 5 3 1

New Directions Books are published for James Laughlin
by New Directions Publishing Corporation
80 Eighth Avenue, New York 10011

HERMAN

The Game Warden

(first version)

The assignment—although exactly what he had been secretly counting on, despite a lurking fear that his retirement might make them decide they no longer needed him—in the end came unexpectedly, one might say caught him unprepared, for at the time when in the plainest terms sparing all empty formalities he thanked the "wildlife management experts for their trust," and accepted their mandate, he had felt almost panicked, as one who reached his goal too easily, practically unhindered, without any struggle, for not only had he "privately counted" on this, but this was in fact what he had been expressly planning when years earlier he had first entertained the idea of retirement, hoping it would bring real liberation and a certain latitude "absolutely necessary for the unimpeded unfolding of his abilities, smothered as they had been by fatuous requirements, rules and regulations." As he himself later recognized there was certainly nothing surprising in his being chosen, though it would have been gratifying to know that it was his well-known perfectionism, endless perseverance and unflinching work ethic that convinced the authorities about his indisputable rightness for the job, but he was aware nonetheless that in selecting him the experts were paying homage to a peerless virtuoso of trapping who — as Herman more than once remarked with bitter irony — was in a way "the last of the Mohicans," guarding the splendid mysteries of an ancient craft gradually sinking into permanent oblivion. Of course beyond the personal considerations the decision was also justified by the nature of the task: the Remete woods in question (a mere couple of hundred acres of hornbeam and oak) had for decades been absent from the forefront of their attention — all forestry activities had been focused on the vast hunting range only five kilometers away—with the consequence that this in-excusable neglect (in Herman's words, "the alarming laxity of the authorities") had turned the Remete by the time of the assignment into an unmanageable and impenetrable jungle, a veritable "sore on the well-groomed body of the region" where no right-thinking hunter or hiker would ever set foot. But the matter had turned really grave only after it was discovered that in this forest left to its fate and gone feral in an almost menacing manner the incredible proliferation of nox-ious predators worried not only the region's farmers but had come to seriously threaten the nearby hunting grounds. A quick decision was made to give Herman a free hand. He plunged into his task and went about his work like a stubborn shadow, "on location" from crack of dawn till late afternoon, clearing scrub, trim-ming trees, building salt-licks and feeders, restoring ranger trails, or, where deemed necessary, blazing new trails; using ancient ways—by reading the tracks lead-ing into and out of the woods—he estimated the numbers of wild stock, both beneficial game and per-nicious predators; relying on intuition and experi-ence, he examined the system of trails usually taken by animals as well as alternate side trails, resting and sleeping coverts, and finally—after it became clear that he would be up against mostly stray dogs and feral cats, as well as a few badgers and foxes—he repaired and de-scented his available stockpile of round traps, steel-jaw traps, dogcatching traps, and, while the local blacksmith, following Herman's clear and precise specifications, fabricated ten of the so-called Berlin swan's necks which, as he repeatedly told the blacksmith, he "expected to work wonders," Herman shut himself up for days in his home workshop making sure there would be no shortage of deadfall traps and snares when the need for them arose. Next came a long period of habituation until the day arrived when Herman felt certain that predators no longer shied away from his well-camouflaged traps and he decided that his plan would "go live" on the morrow. He had no doubts about success, having familiarized himself with the predators' trails, observed the directions of the wind, concocted his own de-scenting mix of ripe fish-heads, intestines, diced giblets and other scraps of offal; he employed artificial scents, a variety of baits and lures, and where needed, built chutes of sticks and stones to guide the animal toward a trap, especially for dog-traps — nonetheless he awaited the results with anxious trepidation, for he believed that in his person "an entire profession stood to be judged ... " and that the prestige, which in the case of a profession such as this has been fading for some time and losing relevance, would now regain its former glory. For the authorities who, by offering Herman this paid position, mostly intended to allay their own consciences without expecting serious results, were surprised to find that after two years the almost frightening primal jungle that the Remete had been was now a bright and wholesome spot of color in the landscape, and the experts could hardly believe their eyes reading the summary report submitted by Herman at the end of two years, although in view of the data they had to agree with Herman according to whom "the population of noxious predators has been reduced to a minimum while the stock of useful game has shown a marked increase." A hastily got-up delegation, sent to express the appreciation of the authorities, found him on location engaged in setting up a deadfall trap in a thicket, but Herman's behavior was so unsociable or, rather, so unfriendly, that they thought it better to defer the matter to a later occasion. And when, accompanied by a brusque, rather flippant note ("No need for this!"), he promptly returned the invitation from the game managers' and hunters' association to their usual mid-year awards event, the authorities wisely decided that it was better not to disturb him until he'd had a chance to get some rest since obviously this was nothing but a case of severe exhaustion which, at his age—and after such prolonged exertions!—was "really not surprising" ... although in fact it was the calamitously oppressive masses of noxious predators exterminated over the past two years that caused Herman to have second thoughts. Toward the end of his second year a horrendous nightmare ambushed him for the first time: he glimpses the carrion pit in the distance ... (which in fact he himself had dug at the outset in a carefully maintained clearing, where he flung the carcasses of dogs and cats, and which had the additional advantage of its pestilental stench exerting an as it were "mesmeric attraction" on the predators that had lately become exceedingly shy) ... then, slowly approaching the pit, he becomes aware of a certain hideous stirring ... he hears frightful, nauseating sounds of slurping and sliding, popping and splaying, until ... at last he must confront in the depths of the pit the enormous putrescent hairy mass of dead meat quivering like jelly ... At this point he would jolt awake bathed in sweat, gasping for breath and staring terrified for minutes on end into the dark, and from then on not a night passed free of this recurring horror which soon began to weigh on him in the daytime as well, until one day in the course of his morning rounds, obeying the hunter's unwritten code of ethics and removing and killing the animals caught by his traps overnight, suddenly all his strength evaporated and for several long minutes he had to look on helplessly at the convulsions of a soiled mongrel in its death throes. As far as that goes he knew numerous ways of killing a trapped beast: for a small animal such as a marten he pressed down the animal's head with a stick and stepped on its chest; with foxes, badgers, cats and dogs (provided they survived the night) he first clubbed them on the nose and then with a firm motion he drove his knife between the skull and top vertebra of the stunned beast, thereby severing the spinal cord. At this point however all of his expertise failed him, he was simply unable to take the decisive—and humane—action; as he stood by the dog in extremis, he himself was stunned at this unexpected paralysis, nervously mopping his sweating brow, now and then spitting to the side, unable to overcome his inexplicable weakness. After this came days and weeks, days and weeks spent in an oppressive, unfamiliar daze; his vision began to deteriorate and his ears rang, at times it seemed he would be totally deaf the next minute, and because some malevolent inner force compelled him to constantly tense his muscles like a dog or cat ready to leap from danger, in the evenings having bicycled home he would collapse upon his bed fully clothed, with aching muscles, totally exhausted. In vain he tried to understand what could have happened to him but remained without a clue. By now he had become utterly incapable of calmly thinking over the calamity that had befallen him and so—at least he would not have to acknowledge his alarming condition—he resolved to throw himself into his work with redoubled effort. He constructed deadfall traps at various suitable spots in the forest but—even as he drove in the struts and measured out and sawed lengths of pine poles—not only did his former serenity and pride abandon him, he now labored persecuted by evil forebodings as if about to be overtaken by suddenly falling darkness. In vain did he shut himself up for days at a time within his lodgings in town, hoping to find peace at last, surrounded by stuffed birds, dilapidated furniture, and antlers mounted on the wall, and it was no use to get dead drunk in the grimy back recesses of taverns on the outskirts—it appeared he was beyond all help. At this point he decided to consult a physician. At first he complained about his liver but it was found to be in "perfect working order"; next he suspected a stomach ulcer, but the physician assured him it was out of the question, his digestive system was flawless. Finally—practically in despair, after laboratory tests and screenings failed to indicate the least disorder—at the doctor's office he confidently announced that "he now felt dead certain about where the problem lay" and pointed at his heart. At this the doctor—who by no means could be charged with not having done everything possible to arrive at a diagnosis—barely suppressed a smile but did not object to further examinations. But the results were dismal, and, when a few days after the exams the doctor cheerfully notified him that "You passed with flying colors! You, sir, have a heart of iron!"—Herman completely lost control, and with an angry sweep of the hand at the flabbergasted doctor, stormed out of the office, swearing profusely. Once more he shut himself up at home, but no matter how hard he tried to hunt down the images produced by his troubled mind, they dispersed like shooting stars until he suddenly realized that the thought of the Remete woods filled him with tremendous longing; he stopped fretting, got dressed, pumped up the bicycle tires that had gone flat, and set out in feverish haste. Evening was falling when he arrived. Even though some half-light remained he groped his way as if blind through the thicket, following ranger trails to their end with bated breath and a peculiar, swaying gait, for even now, no longer fueled by the old ardor, he walked on tiptoes lest some twig crack under his boot heels and frighten the predators setting out to hunt in the darkening woods. He considered it unlikely he would find a catch, since the late November rains of the past few days had most likely completely washed out his traps and the shy beast of prey is careful to avoid such places; and while— mostly with a forester's eyes—he made the rounds of feeders and ranger trails he veered between annoyance and a not quite unpleasant anxiety, seeing that after a mere week or two of neglect weeds were already rampant in the woods, here and there broken branches impeded his progress, and most of his iron traps had gotten rusty. He was aware of an invincible, stifling power already busily attacking his manicured paths and trails from all sides, crushing feeders, moldering the box- and pole traps and settling over the entire forest like some enormous infernal serpentine vine in mockery of the spasmodic human will that endeavors to tone everything, all that is complex and unknowable, down to its own heroic simplicity ... Instead of being frightened and surrendering, Herman felt liberated from his oppressive burden and with great relief he noticed that already life seemed to be returning to him, and the austere combination of decisiveness, determination and a serious penchant for order once more filled his spirit with strength and so there was nothing else left than to get home as soon as possible, dry himself, and sleep through the night so that tomorrow—forgetting the shame of the past few weeks—he could set to work afresh. He was about to leave when, four or five steps from the path, under a bush—in the silvery gloaming of a suddenly appearing moon—he noticed a shadow of unusual shape and mass. Careful not to stumble in the dark he stepped closer and turned on his flashlight. The swan's neck trap that loomed relentlessly skyward had completely escaped his mind. The sight nearly leveled him ... the thought flashed through his mind that the past hour that had just restored his peace of mind had merely been God's cruel and vicious joke, now to crush all the more effectively everything in him that had still remained intact ... and in a flash of despair he buried his face in his hands. The huge male fox with a thick coat of fur had frozen stiff in a most peculiar pose: his tail, butt, and rear legs had come to rest heavily on the sodden ground, and the two upright curved irons that slammed together to catch him by the neck, crushing it (in a single horrendous instant, as Herman was well aware) also lifted the beast's upper body and held it in the air; only the head frozen in a snarl and

18

forelegs resting one on the other in a deathly tame gesture were pointing at the muddy ground, downward,
surrendering, conquered. Herman slowly lowered his
hands from his eyes, his stern countenance unable to
turn away from the bedraggled, fraying body, and now
he could no longer hold it back, that scorching heat
not easy to call by name, for it was an emotion rather
than a taming recoil, now it swooped down on him
and caught him utterly defenseless ... This upwelling
elemental compassion was filled with remorse but at
the same time also with a frightening stubbornness,
that obduracy of the misled which follows in the wake
of a wrong committed in ignorance. The almost phys-
ical anguish that the sight produced in Herman was
presently washed away by the sudden rush of blinding
light that—as if his heart had given a throb—made
him glimpse in a flash his entire life like a landscape;
he was not aware of, for he could not now register, the
perilous furrows of darkness receding into the far distance, and saw only this relentless splendor, this pierc-
ing light as it delivered judgment upon each fallible
act. He overcame his emotions, forced the curved
irons apart, freed the animal, and taking it in his arms,

19

carried it to the carrion pit. With a dull thud the fox landed in the depths, and he was unable to let go of that sound all the way back to town—as a refugee in an enemy zone—bicycling home on the mute streets; he locked the gate and the door behind him, turned on the kitchen light and stood in thought in the redeeming silence under the bare bulb. He envisioned the forest wrapped in thick darkness standing still in the night like a ship at anchor, with shadows scurrying past trees—badgers, foxes, cats, and dogs stalking, lying low ... The next day he collected all of his traps, filled the carrion pit with earth, and for weeks after that slept only by day, roaming the forest by night, and following with an ever deepening attention the hunting ways of beasts of prey, at times half dug-in, observing from a foxhole, at other times tracking fresh trails, or lurking behind brush and scrub, in softly falling snow toward mid-December. And by the time real winter arrived, and Christmas came, he finally understood that he had been living his life steeped in the deepest ignorance, allowing himself to be led by the nose, firmly believing he was obeying the order of divine providence when he had divided the world into noxious and beneficial, while in reality both categories originated in the same heinous ruthlessness that had infernal light lurking in its depths, just as he realized with a pang that it was not a fragile peace, nor the "ancestral commands of the heart" that ruled the human world because all that was merely like some transparent film shielding the pullulating "mass of murderous chaos" below. A burst of compassion thus swept him among the fallen, and this same compassion made him revolt against that loyalty that had till now shackled him to the tyranny of the law, and since he now believed that there had to be a higher law beyond human reckoning, he had crossed the borderline past which—he realized—he would remain forever alone. All this time however he did not know what to do until one early morning, bicycling home on the snowy highway, and re-imagining with a measure of pride the badger's hunting foray recently witnessed, it struck him with a pang that he was "already one of them." Once again he was overcome by the guilt that had in fact been unquellable from the beginning, and now he was certain: he would wreak vengeance. He knew there was no one with whom he could share his burden, for who would understand the train of thoughts that led from his nightmare to this realization ("I must deliver justice"), and in any case he understood that a game warden who feels pity for noxious predators was inconceivable. And so, pretending to carry on his former activities, he ordered more swan's neck traps from the blacksmith, one and a half times the size of the earlier ones, and then set about his work along a carefully laid-out plan of action. He packed up the little that he would need to take, shouldered his two Mannlicher-Schonhauer rifles, locked the door and the gate, and deployed himself in the forest, to build himself a winter shelter in a nearly inaccessible part of the Remete. He made an agreement with the dam-keeper whose house stood about two kilometers away on the bank of the Kőrös that he would buy food from him once a week, then—after making the man promise to not say a word about his presence to anyone—he took the "necessary security measures." He secured the entrance of the path from the highway to the forest with a so-called Selbstschuss consisting of two firearms with reversed locks aimed horizontally at each other, affixed at chest height in a bush on each side of the path, with the triggers connected by a length of strong, transparent fishing line, so that when someone unsuspecting intended to turn into the woods and reached and triggered the line the Mannlichers would go off and the victim would execute himself. This "Selbstschuss" was originally used for big game, primarily bears, but of course Herman had other targets in mind, as he installed at the head of each path leading into the woods one enormous, superbly camouflaged swan's neck, because he feared the authorities would soon descend upon him. For the time being his caution seemed superfluous, since for months the authorities had failed to connect the peculiar events taking place in town with the disappearance of the retired game warden whom the wildlife management association had in vain sought to reach at his home, in order to at last hand over his well-deserved reward, for Herman had "vanished without a trace," then they believed that he most likely must have departed to stay with relatives for the winter months. The first sporadic cases of broken legs did not cause the hospital to notify the proper authorities, until in early February law enforcement got wind of rumors being retailed far and wide about the nocturnal depredations of a maniac at large among the residences of peaceful citizens, or possibly it was some kids too young to realize the gravity of their acts. The investigation soon established that the culprit or culprits were using standard, if extremely dangerous, steel-jawed traps, placed in front of the homes of unwary people with the most perverse cunning and inexhaustible inventiveness, superbly camouflaged so that a person leaving the house in the morning was bound to step in it. The doubtless understandable bewilderment that at first characterized the crime-fighting organs soon ended, as the increasingly frequent incidents were creating panic in town, and a special task force was created for "the earliest possible elimination of the problem." This squad at first focused on finding the perpetrator through the identity of those victims who were hospitalized with severe fractures and contusions, but no connection whatever could be established between the injured gym teacher, tax official, florist, forestry officer, truck driver, tailor, several school children, and finally a butcher, and so the investigation came to focus on the traps. The hunters' and wildlife management associations both denied any responsibility for the traps and brushed aside with a certain measure of indignation the notion of any connection whatsoever between these groups and the perpetrators. However—and independently of this response—it was evident that these devices were, so to say, homemade, and therefore the special task force next took into consideration every workshop and machinist capable of fabricating such items, but without any result. Meanwhile further incidents kept occurring and the perpetrators (by now the unspoken consensus was that it must be a gang) evinced extraordinary skills, since in the face of stepped-up nocturnal patrols they escaped apprehension. By the end of February the task force was working in near despair, when unexpectedly it came upon two important pieces of information: first, outside town, they found the rural blacksmith who admitted having manufactured the objects in question, and even though he could not provide an exact identification since he had not known the person who placed the order, in his opinion "he must have been a hunter for sure"; and second, in response to a notice published in the local paper, the dam-keeper from the banks of the Kőrös presented himself, having decided after much mulling that he "could no longer remain silent" ... He related that he had realized weeks ago that the man behind the events must be the retired game warden who had been buying food from him once a week and who was camped out in the Remete woods. One time he had even asked the man, "I can't say I understand what those people did wrong, but if you must punish them, why do you use these ridiculous traps that can't really do them in?" whereupon reportedly all the game warden said was, as it were admitting culpability, "This is the only way, unless I use my bare hands. I've no other means at my disposal," and then once again he made the man promise to remain silent, and ever since then, as the dam-keeper repeatedly emphasized, he hadn't seen him. After this it was naturally child's play to obtain the wildlife management association's retirement list, and when it came to light that since the end of December they had lost track of Herman, all the pieces came together, and everything was clear as day. As a matter of course they sealed up his apartment after finding that the two Mannlichers, registered in Herman's name, were missing, and, beefing up the task force, they deployed a large detachment around the periphery of the Remete woods. By then Herman had not left his perfectly camouflaged winter quarters for days, halfway dug in, strictly rationing food and eating only once a day, because he no longer trusted the damkeeper ever since the man had realized that Herman was "the trapper," and he had only a week's supply of food left. He'd put on all his clothes under his thick winter coat so he would not freeze, and on top wrapped himself in two blankets; he had grown a beard on his wind-chapped face, and his entire being had as it were metamorphosed over the past two months; breathing with open mouth he sat hunched over, motionless on his bedding made of burlap sacks and scraps of fabric, and if at times he ventured forth, or set out for the town at night, he moved stealthily, without a sound, eyes flashing left and right, and at the slightest suspicious noise he was able to leap into the first available hiding place with a limberness that belied his age. During the past three days however he had not moved, not so much out of precaution, but because he sensed the time had come to soberly think over the events of recent weeks. He felt the need for this all the more because lately, especially since the last trapping … it was if something had broken in him, as if … all of a sudden his strength had abandoned him, the strength that had sustained his sense of justice, and when he heard that his traps had caught several children, he began to suspect that maybe he was "on the wrong scent" … Up till now he had been acting in the belief that he would be the one "who would pay them back for having been misled," having been forced to slaughter with his own hands like "a blind man groping in the dark," but by now—on the third day of his anxious soul-searching—he could no longer keep putting it off: he had to confront the possibility that he might have been wrong, and instead of restoring the "missing order," perhaps he and none other had begun its final breakdown, working from the inside, like a woodworm. A sharp pain stabbed into his shoulders, the darkness where he sat suddenly became frightening, and he now sensed he could no longer master his frantically racing thoughts, whereas that was precisely what was needed first and foremost: to once more create order in the chaos of words flee-ing helter-skelter, forestall this menacing collapse, stem the weakness growing inside him. With eyes glowing inward he stared straight ahead, cowering motionless in a disastrous free fall, having by now given up on his chance to calmly resist this all-obliter-ating power, just as one is unable to circumspectly evaluate the situation while hurling down a steep path with only one's feet for a brake, when running of any kind is no longer possible, given the infernal speed of the downslope. There was no need to respond, for the question already smashed with a single blow his rock-solid resolve and any effort to find words would have been useless, for the lurking awareness that he had committed a wrong that "possibly not even God could forgive" was merely obvious by now, and incontro-vertible, like some long-withheld judgment. He did not even notice the increasingly unbearable burden weighing on his shoulders, for by now he felt that in place of the benumbing heaviness of guilt he had arrived at the boundlessly free space of a shining where everything was clearly visible and the "heart's commands" were distinctly audible ... Shutting his eyes in a lightheaded spell he could already see himself setting foot on the forest's tranquil paths to once more walk down the old ranger trails in the gently falling snow, and in this liberating spaciousness he was at once filled with a deep joy, for he saw a sign of grace in his sudden ability to behold everything with new eyes, the eyes of the sinner who knows that everything that surrounds him carries exactly the same weight ... He was not the least bit surprised to hear the voice squawking from a megaphone nearby, in fact as one perfectly aware of the true meaning of these words ("resistance ... hopeless ... resistance ... "), he stood up nodding, and since he was unaware that a special team of the manhunt had already dismantled the Selbstschuss as well as the traps positioned at the trail-heads, he immediately flipped back the well-camou-flaged door of his lair, the sooner to warn his pursuers of the hidden dangers, and, at the same time as sur-rendering himself, to call attention to "the need for universal compassion" and to have "this announced on the radio as soon as possible." The gigantic and frightening hulk—wrapped in blankets, suddenly popping up from underground, tottering under the weight behind his back, like one all alone barely able to hold up a world about to cave in—abruptly materializing in front of them was so unexpected that the team advancing in a semicircular formation—taken by surprise—instantly opened fire. But Herman, like an indestructible monster, for quite some time refused to topple into the snow, until the shooters suddenly realized that the body riddled through and through was held up in the air only by the hail of bullets.

The Death of a Craft

(*second version*)

contra Yukio Mishima

Had Marietta not received the news that her mother was dying (which would not have been really surprising, it had been forever since she had drifted away from home and became one of us, the old woman has of course severed any and all contact with her), and had she not sent word, asking us to accompany her to that godforsaken small town, possibly we would never have heard of "Herman," this in his unique way rather scary fellow, regarding whom to this day it is not entirely certain whether he had in fact really existed or had merely arisen as an embodiment of craven, inferior fears, and perhaps the affair that back in those days threw us into such a tizzy would have remained forever shrouded in oblivion. Our group at the time—three fellow officers and Zsuzsanna, Berta and Lucy—could not say no to our thrilling and delicious Marietta, after all it was winter, and all of us were in a stifling funk following the fiasco of a grueling, over-elaborate and unconsummated saturnalia where, in spite of the "absence" of some of us, there had been no real risk or actual danger, and so we all embarked on the trip full of expectation, seeing in it *ad esse ad posse* the promise of a chance to stand within the radius of the expiring glance, soon to transcend all boundaries, of an already depersonalized dying woman. As the train, its interior as grimy as the exterior, departed at dawn, the more than two hundred kilometers ahead of us—because of the train's annoying slowness—threatened to be unbearably tedious, so it was small wonder that—weary of the Lowlands desolation rippling past our window: flatland, snow, trees, hamlets, and beyond that, hidden by this mute idyll, the living abomination, of course—sleep soon overcame us, except for Berta and Rudolf who briefly closeted themselves in the toilet at the end of the corridor, until their fellatious amours sent

34

the flabbergasted conductor fleeing when he opened the door asking to see tickets. We were rumpled and spent by the time we got off at the small town's station, and set out across the sparkling, crunching snow toward the hotel on the main square; Marietta alone appeared fresh after the tiresome journey, possibly thanks to the small cookies laced with a mild aphrodisiac she had bolted before arrival that restored her usual vivacity, or possibly because of the keen anticipation of soon being able to see and touch the bed, source and object of her deeply symbolic attachments, where she was born and where her mother now lay dying. Although—as he reluctantly admitted—all of the rooms were vacant, nor, judging by his tormented, hankering glances at our girlfriends, could he have had any objection to our persons, the desk clerk nonetheless showed an incomprehensible resistance, indeed he seemed prepared to dissuade us at whatever cost from staying in town. And so it was well past noon by the time we could occupy our rooms upstairs and pacify Marietta who had insisted with eyes ablaze that we go at once to see the dying woman, until at last we managed to persuade her that after our sleepless night and the fatigues of the journey she had an even greater need for a few hours of rest than we did. Obeying our prior request, the desk clerk knocked on the door of Oliver's room at seven, when, peeking in and catching a glimpse of Berta and Lucy asleep in bed, sweetly entwined, he beat a flustered retreat, returning several minutes later to whisper into Rudolf's ear in the other room: "The manager would like to have a few words with the officer gentlemen." But it seemed that the matter could not have been all that important, because no one disturbed us during dinner in the hotel dining room, and not even when we stepped out of the foyer into the freezing wind did the desk clerk trouble himself to hinder us, but leaning on the reception counter kept nervously chewing his fingernail, and merely sent a shouted warning after us to be careful, work on the street lighting in town wasn't quite completed … Indeed, once outside, we almost fell on our faces, and on the icy sidewalks it surely must have taken us half an hour to cover what otherwise would be a ten-minute walk to the house of Marietta's birth. As we sheepishly entered the room, the acrid smell of perspiration stopped us short in the doorway, and we never did get any closer since the old woman, seeing Marietta, gathered all her remaining strength, grabbed the nurse's arm and implored her in a hoarse voice to drive out of her room "these monsters! Anything," she shrieked, in abhorrence, "but this!" So we slowly backed out of the miasma of sweat, to wait outside at the gate for Marietta, who, we knew, would not calm down until she had touched the aged planks of the bedstead, until her velvety palm clasped "the link connecting her birth and her rapidly approaching liberation." Until Marietta joined us, we exchanged somber questioning glances, for we were unable to decide if we were meant to intervene in the transpiring scene which, we sensed, needed our gifts for its true completion: the bold momentum of sacrilege, the thrilling frisson of a criminal act. That is to say, before catching a glimpse of the old woman taking her terrified leave of the light we had been positive that the occasion — it depended only on us — would offer an opportunity to fulfill the until now stillborn promise of our hand-cuffed imaginations, and since our paraphiliac experiments had been aimed at precisely this impossibility, the total liberation of the imagination — in Gusztáv's words—"from the infernal void of *esse*," it was very hard for us now to renounce this chance of its realization, the tantalizing prospect that perhaps this time we would succeed in emerging into the boundless spaciousness of freedom, from where—even if only for a split second before extinction—we could contemplate the dreadful beauty of our existence. But as Marietta stepped out from the house her gentle, resigned wave of the hand left no doubts that we would not be going back to the death chamber—she was gone for good—and so it was with heads hung in dejection that we returned to our hotel where we sat down rather listlessly around one of the filthy tables of the bar that stayed open all night. We were sitting there undisturbed barely ten minutes when the night waiter with the nauseating smoothness of a sophisticated peasant stepped to Oliver's side and said in a soft voice that the manager requested permission to sit down at our table. Before Oliver had a chance to fend him off, the little mannikin with his toothbrush mustache had already pulled up a chair between him and Zsuzsanna.

*

"I beg the gentleman officers' pardon for intruding," (he obsequiously began) "and let me apologize especially to the ladies," (here he nodded meaningfully in Berta and Lucy's direction) "but I am certain that you won't be angry with me if I can manage to have you hear me out ... For me, especially for me it is most painful to have to speak about this, for after all I am well aware that it is first and foremost the management's task to safeguard the complete comfort of our guests, the perfect tranquility of their days spent here, but it would be a grave and unpardonable error if I were to remain silent any longer about the unprecedented state of affairs that is not quite without danger for our guests who came to our tranquil little town so free of noisy extravaganzas but offering quiet pleasures ..." (He wiped his dry forehead with the handkerchief he clutched, and by now he was halfway off his seat, as one well aware his presence is not welcome.) "It's been already several weeks" (dabbing his still quite dry forehead) "that respectable citizens in our town ... found ... various animal carcasses outside the doors of their homes ... chiefly deer, stag and doe, and pheasant ... but perhaps I am anticipating myself, please excuse me ... if I seem a bit absentminded ... Well then ... we suspect someone criminally insane is on the loose, running rampant, unhindered, at night to terrorize our innocent population with the horrid carcasses of trapped big game and little birds. Alas, it's proof of his extraordinary skill that we have so far failed to catch him, even though," (the manager sent up a weary sigh) "you can believe me, one of the volunteers, we have done everything possible ... Our cause is no better off now that we've found out who is behind these incidents ... it's a ... retired game warden ... named Herman ... about whom, let me assure you, no one would have imagined even six months ago that one fine day ... out of the blue ... he'd become unhinged, and decide to commit such horrors ... Now you, gentlemen officers, might ask, but what is so horrible about this? and, more to the point, where's the danger? Well," (the manager heaved another sigh, cleared his throat, and nervously picked at his mustache) "we have reason to believe that Herman ... poor devil ... will not stop at this, and all of us are convinced that this is just the beginning, and he's planning to do something unprecedented! Because ... these carcasses in front of our houses ... are merely symptoms, warnings ... but what he might be hatching up ... we cannot know for sure ... Naturally" (the manager waved a weary hand) "you now expect me to provide an explanation, what could have set Herman against us. Because that's what this must be about, we are sure of that by now ... But we're still at a loss for answers, we're all in the dark ... no one is able to say anything definite. So in any case" (and here he barely noticeably thrust out his chest), "after all this you will understand if I act against myself and my hotel in asking you gentlemen officers, to take my advice, and leave tomorrow morning, for I must confess I cannot take any responsibility for your party. And now, if you will excuse me ..."

It would probably be stretching the truth if I said that his presence and his rant—beyond the unpleasant sensation created by his strained efforts to choose his words carefully, when obviously he felt like shouting—sparked the least flicker of attention in us, because on first hearing, the manager's muddled story seemed patently absurd and rather ridiculous; but when Oliver gave sarcastic thanks for the "exhaustive briefing," and the manager in turn proposed, as corroborating evidence, that we take a look in a storage space next to the kitchen, where all the carcasses thus far collected were—as he put it—"placed on ice awaiting the final developments, since the authorities have not given permission to either utilize or to destroy them," then, with a modicum of curiosity, we followed the brisk little man, only to stop short on the threshold when the heavy door was pulled wide open. The stone floor was covered by a staggering number of carcasses dumped in a heap, deer and who knows what else, the entire pile topped by a layer of ice. "Well now?" shrilled the manager behind us. "Now do you believe me?!" If nothing else, this fatuous intermezzo served to somewhat revive us after the woeful fiasco of the Marietta affair had frustrated the entire purpose of our trip; we ordered drinks to be sent up and locked ourselves in one room where, after a frenzied session of dalliance (this time Gusztáv handled the whip), we all retired for the night. In the morning, at Marietta's suggestion, we called for the desk clerk to come up and give a detailed account of the current state of affairs in town, and in particular what he himself thought about the peculiar activities of the trapper. In great confusion he hastily pulled the door shut behind him and deflected our request, saying that to his knowledge the manager had given us a detailed account yesterday, and he—as a mere employee—had nothing to add. Only upon Rudolf's peremptory command did he knuckle under and admit, wringing his hands, that the rumors, "as far as that went, were true, but heaven knows why this calamity befell us ..." "It's all right," Marietta encouraged him, "don't be afraid to speak." At this the desk clerk—eyes averted for he dared not look at Marietta who for that matter was still undressed, and her splendid body and dazzling lingerie would have struck him speechless—started to stammer, he wasn't a very fluent speaker to begin with, and he now addressed his words exclusively to Marietta, as if no one else were in the room.

"We simple folk don't understand any of this. But I am scared. And so is everyone." ("Really!" urged Marietta, wrinkling her snow-white brow.) "They say this guy Herman is some kind of fanatic, but no matter what they say, that he's crazy and so on and so forth, don't you believe it, Miss. He knows very well what he's

doing. He's not happy with the way things are." ("What things?" Marietta's bright eyes sparkled at him as she smiled.) "The things going on here nowadays. Because believe me Miss, anything goes here these days. In to-day's world." ("Really now!" prompted Marietta, and drew up her right leg, languidly clasping her hands around it and resting her chin on her knee.) "Around here, Miss ... nothing is sacred any more. It's a godless and lawless world. Folks spend money like water, like there's no tomorrow, you can't imagine what's going on here. Plus everyone's rutting like rabbits. I am a church-going man, I can't say any more." ("Rutting?" echoed Marietta, raising her gorgeous eyebrows.) "That's right. You have no idea, Miss. What goes on here behind closed doors. Our parish priest says it's a regular So-dom and Gomorrah. And he's right." ("And what about this Herman," Rudolf interjected: "Who is he?") "Her-man? Why, he's that trapper. So they say. At first he was trapping only noxious beasts" ("Noxious beasts? What are they?" Lucy tittered) "in the municipal woods, that was his assignment. But now he's trapping useful game. He leaves them on doorsteps. At night. As a warning. A warning to the sinful, Miss. Folks are more frightened by

44

his traps than if he threatened them with a gun. Because that's what's coming next. He will round them up like stray dogs. That's all I can tell you, Miss. Can I go now?" ("But still, what do you say?" asked Marietta, stopping him.) "Who me? I say nothing, Miss. A simple man had better keep his mouth shut. But folks say that he's gone crazy and his deranged mind can't tell what's noxious from what isn't. But he can tell, Miss, he can tell all right. That's what our parish priest says too." ("Tell me, have you ever seen him?" asked Marietta with a lascivious smile, pulling her chair closer.) "Who, the trapper? No, not yet. But they say he's a strapping fellow. And sly as a fox. They can't get the better of him. That's all I can tell you. Now can I go Miss?"

"What a stupid sentimental yokel!" remarked Rudolf, when the desk clerk had scurried out the door, quaking in his boots. Still, he could not deny that he too was amused by the story and so we agreed to stay on until we found out something definite. Following an ample breakfast we spent the next day at the small town's public baths, where—although they had refused our earlier request—upon seeing Berta and

Zsuzsanna, with Gusztáv joining in, improvise a kind of "water ballet" in the nude for our pleasure, the screeching hags on the staff herded out the pop-eyed, obese retirees and let us have the place to ourselves for an hour, in return for a by no means trifling gratuity. In a trice Oliver and Lucy too immersed themselves in the more and more tempestuous rites, leaving only us voyeurs reclining on poolside raffia mats amidst the mounting giddiness, as well as a few chance gawkers glued to the glass door of the entrance, joyless, wretched captives of craven cravings. The evening and night proved uneventful, save for a slight hitch with Oliver, who must have taken an overdose that made him throw up, but by two a.m. he too was feeling better, and retired to bed accompanied by Marietta. By our third day in town we would most likely have forgotten all about the implausible story of "Herman," had the bleary-eyed manager not stormed in during breakfast; rushing to our table, ditching his previous polite act, he could now only gasp, "It's starting!" and left us without further explanation, as if unable to control his agitation. Minutes later, reappearing in a more composed state, he informed us in a somewhat calmer voice that "'Herman' has gone to war": the postmaster's older daughter, a butcher, and the high-school gym teacher all had to be hospitalized today with severe leg fractures, because this morning, leaving for work, they had stepped into large leg-hold traps fiendishly placed in the area between front door and garden gate. "It's starting!" was the manager's parting shot, his eyes feverish as he dashed off at last, tearing at his toothbrush mustache. From then on—in return for a liter of riesling per day—the desk clerk's morning phone calls kept us informed of further developments, and with mounting interest we followed "Herman's" increasingly scary exploits, as night after night he succeeded in placing fresh booby traps in courtyards and streets, at entrances to schools, public buildings, and parks. He used mostly large leg-hold traps and so-called Berlin swan's necks and the desk clerk's morning reports made it clear that in spite of every stratagem the special nocturnal task force organized explicitly for this purpose was unable to apprehend him, because "Herman" operated with extraordinary cunning and was practically invisible, not a soul had been able to catch even a glimpse of him since the start of these events, and so his figure had gradually come to acquire an almost supernatural aura. The supposition, unsubstantiated to the very last, that "Herman" really existed was founded on, beside the acts perpetrated in town, the discovery on the fourth day of our sojourn of traps in the thickets of the municipal woods, obviously abandoned there because he no longer needed them. Among others they found several tilt traps the malevolent ingenuity of which stunned the populace. This was simply a plain wooden crate inside which, on the longitudinal axis "Herman" installed a plank tilting on a fulcrum that worked in the manner of the playground seesaw, that favorite recreation of children, with the difference that when a noxious predator ran up on the plank to reach the bait at its end, the plank tilted under the weight, releasing a catch that snapped the entrance door shut tight, closing off the escape route for good. At least as much consternation was caused by several snares that—as the desk clerk explained—consisted of a simple noose that caught the ground-nesting bird stepping into it, and tightened as the bird struggled to free itself. People chose to see all of this as evidence of a sophisticated cruelty, although it was obvious even to us, unfamiliar with the art of trapping, that "Herman" must be a fanatical professional obsessed by his craft, who relied on ancient traditional methods to build his contraptions. And as the incidents recurred, and the terror if possible grew even more frantic in what was to follow, we too came to look forward with excitement to the desk clerk's news, not that the mounting panic had affected us but because by the fifth or sixth day we all began to suspect that there must be some interconnection between "Herman" and ourselves. We spent days discussing the breaking news (we even got to handle one or two leg-hold traps through the good offices of the manager who apparently was one of the leading figures in the crusade against "Herman"), until we realized with astonishment that whereas our group—or to use Gusztáv's favorite expression: our detachment—as monsters of forward progress was playing the role of pioneers in a world only hesitantly liberating itself from the controlling machinery of goodness, "Herman" had all this while been acting as a fanatic obsessed with the centripetal forces of restraint. And whereas our techniques— having realized in the wake of our sorry experiences that we were not questing heroes but merely dumb victims of the thinking mind—were based on paraphiliac fulfillment, unbridled pursuit of pleasure, the ceaseless apocatastasis of an Eden missing from primal imagination, and took refuge in transgression, Herman's deliberately paltry means were called into being by hubris, a hubris that believed in the invincibility of weakness. We realized that even as we (again only Gusztáv managed to find the right words) brutalized things, violating their frail integrity precisely because of their perfection, "Herman," driven by the pressures of ancient ingrained compulsions, managed to monumentalize destructiveness. After the foregoing, it was understandable why we accepted the hotel manager's invitation when he informed us that for the purpose of apprehending the trapper several so-called public- and self-defense groups had formed in town, and that he felt that since we were well aware of the intolerable situation, we too might take part in the hunt. And so there we were the very same night, the four of us holding our loaded service revolvers with safety off, patrolling the streets, and although we lacked the violent hatred flushing the faces of local citizens, we still searched diligently, turning our heads and firing a few prudent shots at shadows flitting by here and there. It was useless: neither we nor the outraged residents were able to accost the mysterious trapper, and since for several days after that he suspended his activities, it appeared that, recognizing his impotence in face of our overwhelming forces, he would take to his heels. But it did not happen that way, although the havoc he had created ended as natural disasters do: without the citizens' countermeasures attaining their goal, "Herman" himself decided to end his campaign through a peculiar action. One day at dawn, when the Catholic cathedral's deaf pew-opener set out toward the high altar to change the water under the potted plants, he suddenly came to a standstill seeing a frightful object on the red carpet a few steps away from the Crucified One. It was one of "Herman's" swan's-neck traps, presumably: the last one. And since the town understood this to mean their trials were over, the contraption was not removed until that evening, so that every single one of the citizens who flocked there for the spectacle should witness this solemn moment when it became obvious that here was the irrevocable end of an attempt, a profession, an ancient craft. The disquieting question, whether "Herman" had intended the trap for those approaching the altar or perhaps for Christ descending from the cross, was to remain unanswered, because the demon, the ever tormenting, absent antagonist to our heroic struggles, had most likely left town early that morning, never to be heard of again. By now the local residents must have exorcised every trace of his memory, and only we are left to relish the magic bouquet of this escapade, with the exception of our thrilling and delicious Marietta, who has since become the victim of a regrettable accident.

TRANSLATED BY JOHN BATKI

"The excitement of Kraszna[...]
that he has come up with h[...]
there is nothing else like it in contemporary
literature."
— Adam Thirwell, *The New York Review of Books*

"Krasznahorkai is a visionary writer; even the
strangest developments in the story convince,
and are beautifully integrated within the novel's
dance-like structure. It's a testament to Szirtes'
translation that Krasznahorkai's vision leaps off
the page. The grandeur is clearly palpable."
— *The Guardian*

"Most people who have read his fiction invoke the
names of Gogol, Thomas Bernhard and Samuel
Beckett." — Jane Shilling, *New Statesman*

"Shimmers with originality and imagination."
— Eileen Battersby, *The Irish Times*

"Inexorable, visionary—the contemporary
Hungarian master of apocalypse who inspires
comparison with Gogol and Melville."
— Susan Sontag

THE LAST WOLF

László Krasznahorkai

THE LAST
WOLF

EL ULTIMO LOBO

*Translated from the Hungarian
by George Szirtes*

A NEW DIRECTIONS BOOK

Manufactured in the United States of America
New Directions Books are printed on acid-free paper
First published as a New Directions Book in 2016
Design by Erik Rieselbach

Library of Congress Cataloging-in-Publication Data
Names: Krasznahorkai, László, author. | Szirtes, George, 1948– translator. |
Batki, John, translator. | Krasznahorkai, László. Utolsó farkas. English. |
Krasznahorkai, László. Herman, a vadőr. English. Title: The last wolf ;
& Herman : the game warden, the death of a craft / Laszlo Krasznahorkai ;
translated from the Hungarian by George Szirtes and John Batki.
Other titles: The last wolf and Herman
Description: New York : New Directions Publishing Corporation, 2016. |
"Originally published in Hungarian as Az utolsó farkas (The Last Wolf,
originally published 2009), and Herman, a vadőr, A mesterségnek vége
(Herman, originally published 1986)"—Title page verso.
Identifiers: LCCN 2016022374 (print) | LCCN 2016035509 (ebook) |
ISBN 9780811226080 (alk. paper) | ISBN 9780811226097 () |
Classification: LCC PH3281.K8866 A2 2016 (print) |
LCC PH3281.K8866 (ebook) | DDC 894/.51134—dc23
LC record available at https://lccn.loc.gov/2016022374

2 4 6 8 10 9 7 5 3 1

New Directions Books are published for James Laughlin
by New Directions Publishing Corporation
80 Eighth Avenue, New York 10011

THE LAST WOLF

There he was, laughing, but in trying to laugh in a more abandoned manner he had become preoccupied with the question of whether there was any difference at all between the burden of futility on the one hand and the burden of scorn on the other as well as with what he was laughing about anyway, because the subject was, uniquely, everything, arising from an everything that was everywhere, and, what was more, if indeed it was everything, arising out of everywhere, it would be difficult enough to decide what it was at, arising out of what, and in any case it wouldn't be full-hearted laughter, because futility and scorn were what continually oppressed him, and he was doing nothing, not a damn thing, simply drifting, spending hours sitting in the Sparschwein with his first glass of Sternburg at his side, while everything around him positively dripped with futility, nor to mention scorn, though there was an occasional drop in the intensity

7

of this feeling, moments in which he actually forgot about it and stared quite blankly ahead, staring for interminable minutes at a time at a crack or a stain on the wooden floor of the bar, since this was the simplest thing to do, that is after having dropped round the corner, immediately after waking, to start there and end there, not as though he were drinking himself stupid, for after all he couldn't even afford to do that, but rather, as always, out of sheer habit, because at some time he must have said, bring me a Sternburg *bitte*, and ever since then that is what he had been served with, as soon as the man caught sight of him, so he didn't even have to open his mouth but simply step into the Sparschwein and there was the Sternburg ready on his table, not that he took deep draughts of it of course, taking just the odd sip, just enough so he should be able to remain there, as indeed he did remain, generally for two or three hours, and even then he only left the table so as to take a turn round the Hauptstrasse with its filthy sidewalks, down toward Goeben, then out toward the Kleistpark as far as Kaiser-Wilhelm-Platz, where he would cross to the far side by the fishmongers and Humana Second Hand in

order to retrace his steps, the sidewalk horribly filthy because everyone, young and old, was constantly spitting on it as they walked or just stood, but spitting in any case, even when looking into a shop window or waiting for a bus, and that might have been why it all felt so sticky wherever he went, not like a place for walking, because as soon as you set off you feared you'd soon be stuck fast, so you needed to walk at a certain speed, at *brisk walking pace*, as he thought of it, so he shouldn't feel anything, and, what was worse, in the doorways there were pools of vomit that had frozen overnight, and the walls too were filthy with their weather-soaked, spray-painted Kurdish graffiti, and, to put it in a nutshell, the walk started and ended in Hauptstrasse, and there he was laughing, but he didn't read it through the second time, at least he didn't even touch the letter for a while, for how stupid it was, he told the Hungarian barman though the man simply stared at him, quizzically raising his eyebrows, not listening, not even hearing because the music was so loud, an especially sugary piece of Turkish pop, the kind continually being played in the Sparschwein, by either Mustafa Sandal or Tarkan, or Tarkan or Mustafa

Sandal, the choice of music being hard to explain because it was pointless the owner trying to lure customers into the bar with it, a bar selling alcohol, since the Turks tended ever more to wander in by mistake, but what the hell, he waved his hand, and looked out through the window though there was nothing worth looking at out there just some drug dealers leaning against the wall by the Sparschwein, waiting for something, the sky leaden, nothing to see, all aspects of futility and scorn, he thought, pushing the letter away from him because he didn't even feel much like screwing it up and throwing it into the nearest litter-basket, the whole thing a nightmare, he told the Hungarian barman, and laughed, but the man was paying no attention at all now, though even if he were there would have been no point in trying to explain things by saying it was some ridiculous advertisement or that it had been misaddressed to him because it was serious, and therefore impossible to misaddress, yes, serious indeed, extremely serious as it turned out, and it was just that the whole business was utterly ridiculous, because while it had in fact been addressed to him, and was genuinely from Madrid, he can't have been the

one it was intended for, since he wouldn't have been invited to Extremadura, by this unheard-of foundation, a foundation staffed by people he had never heard of, asking him whether he felt like spending a couple of weeks there writing something about the region, and what was this with "felt like"?! hadn't he been living here for years, here in the embattled wasteland of the Hauptstrasse, earning three hundred Euros from one or two lectures, which was just enough to see him through on a day by day basis, so it must clearly have been a mistake which might be explained by them having sent the invitation a few years ago (it would not have been unusual for the local post office that he should have just received it) or it might be that they didn't know that the person they were inviting no longer existed, that, yes, there had been someone of that name some time in the past, the name right in that sense, but that there wasn't anyone behind the name now, no "Herr Professor," and while it was possible that some such title did once precede his name it had made no sense for several years now since there was nothing, not a thing, to connect him with a person who, while he existed, was unaware that there was

no point in thinking, who had written a few unread-
able books full of ponderously negative sentences and
depressing logic in claustrophobic prose, a series of
books in fact, when it had long became obvious, almost immediately obvious, that no one read them of
course, and, that being the case, he must long have
been washed up as a philosopher, no one was making
any serious attempt to understand him or what his
sentences, his logic, his diction or prose might be
about, and in the meantime he had practically no in-
come, which made it impossible for him simply to
give up, and they said they would pay all his expenses,
his flight, the cost of his accommodation and provide
a car as well as an interpreter, all "awaiting you on arrival in Madrid to drive you over to us in Caceres or
Badajoz, where we could offer you a fee of X Euros for
your article," this being something he couldn't get out
of his head, so he would sit on his bed with the letter
in his lap imagining what he could do with so many
Euros, and how it was exactly like having your name
drawn in a lottery, meaning, you, yes you; you, if anyone, can't afford to reject such an offer, and you have
only to do this and that thing, the whole thing being

an absolute bloody nightmare, he muttered to himself, staring out of the window, seeing only himself, an enormous mirrored bald pate, the next day having started just like the previous one, waking with difficulty then getting down to the Sparschwein, the taste of cold Sternburg in the cold bottle, the usual thing and the Hungarian barman, who, he felt, was his most intimate companion, one who nevertheless never once succeeded in putting the glass gently down before him, a failure that exacerbated his already terrible nervous state, a state that was hard to explain, but he would happily have smashed the bastard's face in, because why go slamming it down on the table every time, with the sky so overcast outside, a leaden sky yielding little light, the drug dealers leaning against the wall, the sidewalk sticky with spittle and that bitter taste in his mouth of futility and scorn as he drifted down toward Goeben than the Kleistpark followed by Kaiser-Wilhelm-Platz, then over to the other side, past the fishmonger and the Humana Second Hand store thence back to the Sparschwein, where he did not throw the letter away, it still being tucked in his pocket, but read it through, for it really was addressed to him,

he really was the person being addressed, he had established that much, and had in fact begun faintly to
believe it, at least believe it more than he had done the
previous day, trusting that it was no mistake and never
had been because he had received an immediate con-
firmation in response to the e-mail he had sent from
one of the tables in the Telecafe next door, a response
that confirmed that they were indeed expecting him
and asked when he would arrive, adding that he was
welcome to stay as long as he wanted, though he still
didn't quite believe it, he muttered to the Hungarian
barman in the Sparschwein, and set off down the
sticky sidewalk of the Hauptstrasse trying to accustom
himself to the thought that at any moment he could
fly off to Extremadura, though he had no idea where
"Extremadura" was, having just two acquaintances in
Spain, his selfless one-time translator and his selfless
one-time publisher, though even they, naturally, had
been obliged to pulp his books because they couldn't
sell them, as a result of which his connection with
them was long lost, that being about the time he lost
contact with everyone else, though this remained the
one possibility, to write to them and ask them what

was going on? what was this invitation? "believe it or not" and whether it was real at all, this "Extremadura" that had once been what the Romans called Lusitania, so he went to the Telecafe, and there came the answer: yes, Extremadura was the modern Spanish part of the ancient Lusitania, which is to say the province was partly located in modern Portugal, with Andalusia beneath it and Castila y Leon above it, and it was from there the Conquistadores set out but all the same, the ex-translator and ex-publisher asked—and you could sense their astonishment—how was it that it should be precisely him, he who had long been known to carry a vast store of information in his head, that he could be confused about such things, how far had he fallen from his eminence, the message being plain, quite plain from their replies, that this was what they were asking themselves, and, all the same, were asking him, there, in capital letters talking about it, meaning, what the hell would you be doing in Extremadura, because THERE IS NOTHING THERE, it's just an enormous, mercilessly barren, flat place, with a few small hills generally near the border, horribly dry, the hills bare, the earth dried out, with hardly any people

since life was as hard as it could be there, serious poverty, an utterly parched place, why the hell go to Extremadura, when you could come and visit us in Barcelona, his two warmhearted philosophy-loving friends exhorted him, Barcelona being a proper place, but no, he told the barman who was looking cross because, despite having turned down the volume on the cassette player, he still couldn't understand what his customer wanted, no, he was going to Extremadura and if there wasn't much there then it would suit him down to the ground, he wouldn't look out of place himself, that's if the invitation was for real, for he was constantly in doubt about everything to the extent that he started worrying about it all over again, looking out at the drug dealers, staring at the floor, at the bar, repeating to himself the word, Extremadura, then sending another e-mail to which the answer was even plainer than before, and so it must all be true, he told the Hungarian barman, who asked: what is true? at which point he shrugged, saying, never mind, then gestured for another bottle, the sum being such and such amount of Euros, a melancholy sounding such and such amount, and so he watched the passersby,

16

noting the way they spat, mumbling "a fortune" to himself in front of the big bicycle repair shop window, then writing to the Badajoz center from the Number 2 machine of the Telecafe next door to say that 21 February would be fine, a date he happened to pick because he could have written the 22nd or the 24th or chosen March or even April, or anything really, but had pressed Enter on the grubby computer to confirm the 21st February, carefully adding the tag, "I could stay for a week" to which came the reply, "Excellent!" from Extremadura, "we will send you the ticket immediately," (the ticket arrived), and, "we await your arrival, and once you have arrived you will be provided with an interpreter, a car, and anything else you need" and he was already on board the airplane when the weight of something in his head began to pull two opposite ways at once for it was clear the whole thing had been his mistake, either that or they had mixed him up with someone else, to which he added the possibility that the person they were confusing him with was in fact him, it was just that that particular "him" no longer existed, so there he was, as he explained to the Hungarian barman once he was back in Berlin,

watching as the plane made its descent to Madrid, where they immediately recognized him from the description he had given of himself, a task not too difficult considering his 120-kilo body weight, his facial appearance and the blue zip-up jacket he was wearing, he said, pointing to himself, just as it was not too difficult recognizing the middle-aged woman who was to act as his interpreter, who greeted him at Arrivals with a broad smile on her face and a board with his name on it raised high above her head, his name, yes, though all the way on the bus he kept thinking that even if they had been thinking of him it wasn't actually to him the invitation had been extended, and all the while the buildings of Madrid were speeding by and he occasionally nodded at something the interpreter said who, it seemed, wanted to out-shout the protesting voice within him and was practically bellowing, trying to explain something to him in English, something that took the whole long route to Caceres to explain, but of which he only caught the essential part, that being that she, his interpreter, was waiting for Herr Professor to tell her what he would like to see and what he would like to write about, since they could get

18

started the very next day if he felt like it, and Herr Professor—do keep to the point, the Hungarian barman grumbled—but he had stopped listening because he really couldn't bear someone shouting in his ear like that, and in any case, he had not the faintest notion how to confess to her that, of course, he couldn't write about anything, for really, what could he possibly do with his hopelessly complex, labyrinthine thoughts and sentences, but never mind, he thought, and watched through the bus windows as the fields rolled past, the whole thing, the entire set-up, was of no interest whatsoever since sooner or later it would become obvious that it had been a mistake to invite him, as a result of which he spent the first few days always coiled, always tense, always waiting for someone to come up to him and quietly admit that, yes, it had been a mistake inviting him, and that they'd be taking him back to the airport now, asking him not to make them look ridiculous again, but the fact was no one came to upbraid him about that, not in the first few days, nor in the last, on the contrary, they treated him as though he were an international celebrity—well, naturally, the barman nodded irritated as he stacked

the glasses—but really, he insisted, like a celebrity, with the finest hotel, magnificent dinners and suppers and the constant, never-ceasing encouragement to feel free, to do just what he wished to do, to travel north or south or east or west just as he pleased, and the car and driver are always at your disposal, as ditto the interpreter, entirely at your disposal, and all we ask is that you immortalize the experience, immortalize it entirely as you see fit, just so long as you present posterity with some clear picture, something that springs out of your thoughts about Extremadura, so you see we are perfectly clear about what we would like you to do, they assured him, we only ask that someone as well known as you—as me? he pointed to himself, terrified, blushing in confusion—but of course, they repeated and smiled, as well known as you, that you, might think about Extremadura, and that, arising out of your thoughts and experience of Extremadura, you might write, might, as we say, give voice to the flowering of Extremadura, this once historical wasteland, this centuries-old nest of human misery that has set out on a new path, a new chapter in its story, and that

is all we want, they smiled and looked straight into his eyes, that is what we are working to achieve, said the people at the foundation, everyone inordinately friendly, all looking to be of service to him, just waiting for him, their guest, to say something or ask for something, because they all wanted to be useful to him, it was just that there was nothing for them to help him with, because the very moment he realized what they wanted of him, which was to help them in their great project which was the writing of the flowering of Extremadura, and that they were anxiously waiting for him to think of something, he lost all sensation and was unable to think at all, not any thoughts whatsoever, that is if his mind was working in the first place, made all the worse by his consciousness of the fact that he should be thinking something, but what? so he sat in the comfortable armchair of the elegant hotel, as he explained to the Hungarian barman, sitting there, gazing at the touching sight of Caceres outside while a terrible burden of helplessness settled on him, for there was nothing there, nothing, he had finished with thinking, and either he was being obliged to

reach back to a time before thinking stopped, though that was a time beyond expressing now, or was expected to employ such remnants of thought as remained, remained, that is, after the thinking ended which necessarily meant silence again since the language at his disposal was no longer capable of giving form to subjects that could not be fixed because it had gone full circle, had articulated all it could possibly articulate and had reached the point from which it had started and was completely exhausted by the circular journey, so how was he to tell these generous, enthusiastic people that the act of thinking for him was over, once and for all, that there was no sense of adventure, no capacity for action left in him, and that, all things considered, he lacked the inner reserves he would need to draw on, nor did he have the necessary range or scope, and that, in short, nothing remained of him but a primitive urge demanding, I WANT, in language as befouled as dirty laundry, he thought, which was precisely the thought that had ruined him, that had been the cause of his failure, the reason for his descent down the slippery slope of futility and scorn these last few years, a descent from the height of an academic

chair to the depths of impersonal dreariness at the Sparschwein, because if he declared, categorically declared, that language itself was wholly corrupt, then it would be self-evidently true that there was nothing worth talking about, either because of the way he didn't talk about it, or because of the way others did, that is by denying that nothing, not even philosophy, existed any more, insisting that it had stopped existing, apart, that is, from the kind of philosophy you might find—if you *could* find it—on displays in the windows of bookshops or on the actual shelves of bookshops, that is to say a pile of old rubbish, nothing but pretense, nothing but mask, nothing but motley, a bunch of repulsive lies if only because everyone was obliged to cover up the fact that these books were usurping the places that should have been occupied by real books, genuine works of philosophy, and, besides, he had never been "a well-known figure," just someone who had tried his luck thinking but had failed—and who could possibly have guessed that? the Hungarian barman wryly observed, but only over his shoulder so to speak, because he was fully engaged in arranging the bottles on the shelves by the wall—

and so my achievements added up to nothing, he continued, and it would have been better, both here and there, in Extremadura, that I be exposed, or revealed in my true colors, but no, that was simply not the way things worked out, I couldn't just go and tell them the truth because they were far too kind, much too nice to be disappointed, and in any case when he did try, there on that very first day, to explain, the interpreter immediately raised her voice and bellowed even more loudly, and he couldn't get a word in edgeways, so failing that, afterward, he suggested, as quietly as he could, that they drive on, that everything was fine, and that they should get going and visit, say, the place where the Arab immigrant *gästarbeiters* lived, at which point the interpreter dropped her voice a little, just a little, and answered enthusiastically, almost triumphantly, as if she had been prepared for just this request, that Herr Professor must be thinking of Navalmoral de la Mata or Talayuella, that they were already on the road to Navalmoral, Navalmoral de la Mata, and good, he said and fretted, what to do, because he had no idea, as he now explained, no idea whatsoever where the place was or why they were going there,

though he tried to concentrate all his attention on the matter and recall what he had read in the Telecafe in the days before setting out, though all he could remember was something about a certain tension among the Arab immigrant workers referred to in some article on ecology in which the two authors cited someone whose name he had written down but couldn't remember where, who reported that "it was south of the River Duero in 1983 that the last wolf had perished" and it might have been the unusual tone of the sentence that stuck in his memory, since scientists didn't tend to write quite so poetically in articles of this sort, did they? didn't tend to talk in terms like "the last wolf" he explained but the Hungarian barman had stopped listening again because a delivery had arrived with consignments of beer, wine, spirits and non-alcoholic drinks and the barman was obliged to count the bottles and check off the list in his notebook, all there, present and correct, the delivery men granted a beer on the house before leaving, so when the barman returned to his position behind the bar and raised his head indicating that he could continue, he continued enthusiastically, saying that something did after all

happen to come to mind on the road to Navalmoral de la Mata, something he had thought about that article, about how scientific articles were quite different because scientists didn't use terms like "perished" or "the last," but never mind, he said, and quickly forgot it in any case as the car proceeded toward Navalmoral de la Mata, the sky cloudless, the temperature pleasantly warm as air blew in through the wound-down car window, the highway quiet with hardly anyone to be seen, while on the way back, by the time he had discovered Arabs really did live in Navalmoral de la Mata and Talayuella but that there was no tension, the tension being further south, in Andalucia, as the locals explained to the interpreter, adding that while there were relatively few here, just a few thousand working during the year, they lived in relative harmony with each other as well as with the native inhabitants of Extremadura, since working in the tobacco fields involved tough discipline and they were pretty well paid for it, and to put it in a nutshell, it was growing dark on the way back so there was literally no one around, so he was no longer thinking about either Navalmoral or Talayuella but about the article, the hum of the car

having made him drowsy, the interpreter herself asleep next to the silent driver, and he remembered that the strange thing about the article was not only the way the oddly poetic sentence stood out in the text but that anyone would know when "the last wolf" had died, for how would anyone know, and, beyond that, the verb itself, "perished" for did any scientist speak like that? no, there was something not quite right about the article, about the sentence, and it was this that had caught his attention as he told the people from the foundation next day at supper in Caceres (via the interpreter) thinking nothing of it, but then they understood him to be suggesting that this should be their task, a problem for them to solve, that he was asking them to find out what article it was Herr Professor had been reading, and, having located it, to track down the text the authors had been citing, the only thing they did not understand being the reason the Herr Professor seemed to be so depressed, the reason he was staring into space in the bar after supper, though they also might have noticed, he told the Hungarian barman, that he would have liked to have told them why, but what could he say, how could he make

them understand what Hauptstrasse was like, what it was like living in Hauptstrasse, what a morning in Hauptstrasse was like, what the Sparschwein was like—so what is it like then? the Hungarian barman growled at him but he didn't answer and simply continued—for how could he describe what so weighed him down, how could he explain how long ago he had given up the idea of thought, the point at which he first understood the way things were and knew that any sense we had of existence was merely a reminder of the incomprehensible futility of existence, a futility that would repeat itself *ad infinitum*, to the end of time and that, no, it wasn't a matter of chance and its extraordinary, inexhaustible, triumphant, unconquerable power working to bring matters to birth or annihilation, but rather the matter of a shadowy demonic purpose, something embedded deep in the heart of things, in the texture of the relationship between things, the stench of whose purpose filled every atom, that it was a curse, a form of damnation, that the world was the product of scorn, and God help the sanity of those who called themselves thinkers, which was why he longer thought, had learned not to think any more,

28

not that this led anywhere, of course, because wherever he looked, whichever way he turned, there was that all-pervasive stench, the stench that was there because the last word, the word that comprehended the knowledge that futility and scorn, replete with purpose, was coextensive with the world, *was* the world, was something of which he had to be conscious, an eternity of futility and scorn that obtained in each and every second of life for those who had set out as thinkers, futility because as soon as you abandoned thought and tried simply to look at things, thought cropped up again in a new form, a form from which, in other words, there was no escape whatever man thought or did not think, because he remained the prisoner of thought either way, and his nose was deeply pained by the stench of it, so what could he do except console himself with the thought that events simply followed their own natural course, which is what happened in Extremadura too, that is to say he let things follow their natural course when next day the eternally jolly director of the Badajoz-based foundation rang to inform him that the article had been found, because he couldn't tell him that he hadn't in fact been looking for

it, that it really made better sense to leave the article where it was and to let events take whatever course they wanted to take, and in any case that was exactly how things turned out since they discovered that the writer referred to in the article by the young co-authors was easy enough to trace, that being a certain Fernando Palacios, one Professor Fernando Palacios, whose telephone number in Madrid was already in their possession and whom, so the message continued, they had immediately tried to contact though so far without success, as they insisted on informing him every ten minutes as he traveled in the car, though by this time the interpreter had taken over the role of the official in Badajoz and had just rung the appropriate number from her position in the back seat even as they were approaching the wonderful valley famed for its flowering cherry that, it had been recommended, "the visitor should see even a month before the cherry trees of the Jerte region begin to blossom" and was soon excitedly pointing to the telephone to indicate that she had succeeded in getting through, that he was "on the line," an announcement that was followed by some animated conversation complete with exclama-

tions of "si, señor" and "gracias, señor" to indicate that
the wolf had been located—really?! asked the barman, his face for the first time showing a flicker of
genuine interest—but no, he answered, not in the
sense that they had tracked down the wolf, just that
they had discovered when and where it had existed,
but then the interpreter yelled that Professor Palacios
would immediately ring back because he said he actually knows the name of the man who shot the last wolf,
though at least an hour went by before the telephone
rang again with more cries of "si señor" and "gracias,
señor," but this time, the interpreter announced in tri-
umph, raising a scrap of paper with a name on it, her
face red with excitement, he really does have it, the
hunter being one Antonio Dominguez Chanclon, and
here's his address and telephone number, and she was
already dialing it, he explained to the Hungarian barman, a truly happy woman, at which point the barman
asked why she was so happy, and he answered that it
might have been because she was pleased to have been
able to help, but the barman didn't understand—it
seemed he had some problem understanding the
whole story, as if he hadn't heard the beginning of it

over the saccharine wailing of Mustafa Sandal, or had missed a vital word in the discourse without which the whole was incomprehensible, though he did provide a running commentary composed of doubt or simply natter on about what he did hear, despite of the fact that there were moments when nothing, not a word, of his commentary could be heard from behind the bar, though that was no problem because his most important dialogue was exclusively with the glasses and bottles, the dishwasher and the tea machine—and so whatever he occasionally said was addressed to them and to them only, and even then only in Hungarian, not to him, not to the man who carried on with his account of how, according to Professor Palacios, he, that is to say Chanclon, had shot the wolf, a male of the species, in 1985—not 1983!—but on February 9, 1985, and that the said Chanclon lived at 3, Avenida Virgen de Guadalupe on the third floor in Caceres, that the incident having occurred at Cantillana la Vieja, near Herreuela, though, according to Palacios, or so the interpreter explained in a state of excitement, it was not precisely there but on a *finca* going under

the name of La Gegosa—on a what? asked the Hungarian barman who really did not like the word—a *finca*, he said, the local name for a private estate where everything is fenced off and the whole territory is surrounded by barbed wire, the estate being protected by wardens or special guards, or both, who make it very difficult to encroach on such an estate—but, he raised his hand in warning, we are still on the subject of Professor Palacios—the subject of who? the barman asked, mystified—a question he ignored with a dismissive wave and continued, saying, this was the information we received in the car, and it seemed it would be smooth going from then on, we'd ring up this Chanclon character, and all would be solved, though what it would all add up to, of course, he had no idea then, though one thing was perfectly clear, this being that there really was a hunter who had really shot a wolf and that since then, as the article stated, there have been no wolves south of the river Duero, there remained only one problem, which was that the telephone very soon rang again, the interpreter silently mouthing the word, Palacios and signaling for

silence, a redundant gesture since no one happened to be speaking and the driver was generally silent anyway, this while he, he pointed to himself, was just digesting the information he had just received and was thinking, good, at last we know how the thing happened, or rather, how they shot the last wolf, but whether he could seize upon this piece of information and make any use of it seemed unlikely since he was incapable of seizing anything or making anything of anything, he reflected, deciding that this had gone far enough and that this very evening he would stand before the people from the foundation and tell them, tell them that … that he wasn't going to write anything, because he was incapable of writing, because being incapable of thinking he was incapable of writing either, neither about Extremadura, nor about the last wolf, the story of which seems to have been entirely true as had been proved by the telephone conversation, though the facts as they came to him now were as follows, and he dropped his voice a little and allowed a moment's silence in which to sip his beer, the fact being that the last wolf was not the one in the Chanclon story, because there were two at that time,

one at Santiago de Alcántara and another near Rio Zapato, and that these two "perished" at much the same time, both being regarded as "the last wolf," in other words that the whole "last wolf" business was a bit of a myth as Palacios admitted to the interpreter on the phone, since all we can say scientifically is that Chanclon's was the last officially registered incident regarding the legal shooting of a wolf, beyond which little can be ascertained with any confidence, little or nothing, information the interpreter passed on, and with that the matter was closed for that day at least, and they parted in the hotel that evening having resolved to ring Chanclon early next morning and to take matters from there, because, for the time being, the interpreter informed him, no one was picking up the phone at his end, though the next morning, she gave him an assuring look to indicate that they were sure to find him in, and yes, he agreed, the next day, because he did not want to bother with it tonight and was happy to wait to see how things turned out, to see what became of Chanclon and his story, and that since everyone at the foundation had been working so hard to locate this Chanclon, he wouldn't tell them there was no

point tonight, but would wait till tomorrow, and so retired to his room where he could hardly sleep for anxiety, thinking that, very well, by tomorrow they would have contacted Chanclon but what about what happens next, because he had no idea, and soon he was feeling positively angry with himself for having accepted the invitation but especially for not having made his situation clear before, because things were getting ever more complicated, and here he was, in the finest hotel in Caceres, and therefore in Extremadura, all the while knowing he would be incapable of writing anything about Extremadura, that he was here under false pretenses, that he was conning people who did not deserve to be conned, people to whom he owed this magnificent visit, this whole, yes, magnificent experience, for however impossible it was for the attractions of the place to distract him from his profound depression, he had to admit, though he had only been here two days, that Extremadura did have a special magic all of its own and that he was almost entirely under its spell; that up to a point, under the cover of his own depression and bad conscience, even he was conscious, he told the Hungarian barman, of

the natural history of Extremadura, which was perfectly wonderful and that he, to take but one example, was especially keen on the *dehesa*, that gently rolling landscape with its own species of oak, the holly oak, that they called *encina*, that was not planted in dense patches but—and this was the whole point—lightly sprinkled around the fields, the various trunks and branches of individual trees maintaining a decent distance from each other on account of the aridity, as the hitherto silent driver explained when he was glossing the word *dehesa*, the dryness of the soil, the oaks being able to prosper only this way for lack of enough water, this way alone, and he pointed through the window at the lack of shrubs and other low vegetation, at the pale soil with its sparse grass and stray oaks on the vast plain, that being the *dehesa*, you understand, as indeed he did understand, and felt inwardly, since the *dehesa* was much like his own soul—like what?! grinned the Hungarian barman—okay, forget it, he waved and took another sip of his beer, all he meant was that Extremadura was marvelous, and not only on account of the natural landscape but because of the people, he explained to the Hungarian barman, the

best way of describing them would be simply as good people, at which the barman raised a skeptical eyebrow, as if to say "good people?!" and, yes, he replied, good people, and that too was marvelous he stressed, only it would be awful telling these good people the fate that awaited them, the *autopistas*, the suburban developments, in Caceres and Placencia, in Trujillo and Badajoz and Merida where he had already been shown how quickly this kind of thing can happen and was all too aware of how the world would break in on Extremadura too, because he knew, and he leaned forward in his chair, raising his voice a little so the barman should hear this much at least over the mechanical bawling of the music, because he knew that the whole place, Extremadura, was outside the world, because *extre* means *outside, out of,* you get it? and that was what was so wonderful about both the land and the people, and that nobody was really aware of the danger presented by the proximity of the world, that they, the Extremadurans, lived in terrible danger because, he explained to the barman, they had no idea what they were letting themselves in for, what spiritual

changes would be set in motion once the *autopistas* and shopping centers had laid havoc to their fields, fields where the poverty had been terrible, because he had seen photographs of what it used to be like and it was dreadful, really dreadful, and one really did have to put a stop to that, and they had put a stop to it, and would continue putting a stop to it, the only dreadful thing being that they had only one way of doing that, and that was by letting the world in, thereby admitting the curse, because everything would be cursed, everything in Extremadura, the land, the people, all, though they had no inkling of it because they lacked the knowledge and had no sense of what they were doing, what they were in for, but he, he did feel it, he pointed to himself, was keenly aware of it and couldn't sleep because of it but lay tossing and turning in the elegant hotel room, worrying about how to face the people from the foundation, because they wouldn't understand but would wonder what he was up to, he was sure of that, and he wouldn't even find the right words, so the next day arrived and everything continued precisely as before, he didn't tell them, told them nothing,

and they were already in the car with the silent driver, already driving away from Caceres because the foundation had in the meantime — at night perhaps? — discovered that Chanclon was no longer living in the town center but had moved to a house at the edge of town, as indeed he had, and he turned out to be a small, charming, talkative man who kept striding up and down the yard, they having spotted from a distance, even from the highway, since it was obvious that he was anxiously waiting for them, but only because, or so it turned out, he was worried in case they were late when there was only just time enough for the meeting anyway since, as he told them, he had to be off somewhere at noon and had had "to snatch this brief hour," so brief that he immediately led them into his little tumbledown house that comprised only a tiny kitchen and one other room, though what faced them in that room, the moment they entered it, was one vast glass case in which the last wolf was displayed, its four legs splayed out — "what!?" gasped the Hungarian barman leaning on the counter, the time being about eleven in the morning or maybe not even

that, with no one else in the bar, the Sparschwein tending to be pretty empty at such a time, so there was not much to do except lean on the counter and wait for something nice, or to listen to this Stammgast, this regular, who was not a proper Eastern European, not even a decent-looking chick, both of which he would have preferred to listen to, but this would do in the meanwhile, so he cleared his throat and you could see he was trying to look poker-faced, not to betray what he was thinking, but carry on, carry on, he encouraged the other in words and with gestures, I see — so there was this enormous wolf in a glass case — and then? — that's all there was and it was quite incredible, that here, in this little ruin of a house, there should be this enormous glass case with a terrifying monster inside, its jaws wide open, because somehow one felt it wasn't quite the right place for it, not in such a house, for how to put it? it didn't seem right that this extraordinarily regal specimen should be there, in that enormous glass case, with the cheery figure of Chanclon beside it, who, as I told you, had told us that he was very pleased to help despite the fact that he was in a hurry

which was why he got straight into a story that he must have told hundreds of times before, probably using the same words, the very same words he would use next time he had to tell the story, explaining that it was getting on toward night and he was on a hillside, under cover, hidden from every direction, the gun in his hand, watching for boar or deer but there had been nothing for hours, when he lit his lighter, this very lighter—he pointed to the precisely placed plastic lighter at the bottom of the glass case—to light his cigarette and got a fright because there behind him, no more than three or four meters off, stood a wolf, the wolf upwind, the wind strong, in conditions of total silence, which might be why the animal failed to notice him despite being so close, Chanclon himself hardly daring to breathe, but then he lit the lighter and they both got a fright, then everything happened incredibly fast, the wolf sensing danger was rushing off and had made about ten or fifteen paces away to one side of him when he pressed the trigger, and honestly, he was really shitting himself, hardly aware of where he was firing, aiming at nothing in particular, not a thing, just letting fly in mere panic, practically shitting

himself, Chanclon explained with a broad smile, just
firing the gun, but he got it, possibly through the
heart, though it didn't fall immediately, only once it
was about a hundred meters away, said Chanclon on
his haunches now before the glass case, and silently
pointed to the wolf's heart, so they all, the interpreter,
the driver, all of them also got down on their haunches
staring at the wolf's heart, though nothing now remained of the wound of course, Chanclon explained,
since it had been perfectly "restored," and there the
great predator stood, baring its teeth, its feet splayed,
frozen for eternity, listening to the tale of its own de-
mise, in the same words, precisely the same words as
it had heard so often before, and he, he pointed to
himself, suddenly felt that the two, Chanclon and the
wolf, genuinely belonged together, because it was not
only the proud hunter who stood there, visibly swell-
ing with pride and pointing out his prey, but it was as
if the pride emanated equally from both of them, from
hunter and hunted, that they were part of the same
thing, he thought, and was explaining this when—listen! the barman interrupted him, then, using the *du*
form, saying, "you ever been to Estreize?" and gave

him a really suspicious look as if he weren't expecting an answer because he already knew the answer would be no—and he himself had no wish to insist that, yes of course, he had, but continued, saying that they were on the road to Valencia and that by this time it was not only the driver but the interpreter who had fallen silent, she having probably been tired out by the visit to Chanclon's, in any case there was silence in the car, a pleasant benevolent silence, and he was preparing himself to see the place Chanclon had been talking about, because that was what had been decided, that was why they were heading from Caceres to Valencia, that's about fifty kilometers out, so that they might find the entrance to the *finca* named Cantillana de Vieja—the what? the barman gave him an angry look because he had forgotten what he had been told about what the word meant—the word *finca*, you know, he explained, a plot or estate guarded by gamekeepers or private security people, the whole mountain, the whole of the Sierra de San Pedro, since that was the name of the mountain, being entirely fenced round like a large estate, you understand—yes of course I understand the barman retorted furiously slapping

the counter with his wiping-up cloth — so it wasn't long before they reached the *finca*, but it wasn't the Cantillana de Vieja, there being no vehicle access there, but the neighboring Cantillana de Nueva where there was at least a parking space, from where they shouted as loud as they could because the house stood some two hundred meters off, and eventually some-one meandered out to see to them this being, as it turned out, Alfredo, the gamekeeper, who listened to the interpreter's account initially with skepticism, ask-ing what it was we were calling about, but then point-ing to the neighboring Cantillana de Vieja, saying that that was the place they wanted, that was where the wolf hunt, the *lobería*, took place, a while ago now, but why? do you remember? asked the interpreter, and, well of course, Alfredo replied slowly nodding, and soon enough they knew as much as he did, since Al-fredo went so far as to draw a map of the estates in the sand for them, to show where the various *finca*s lay, where the old railway used to run, and where, in rela-tion to those, the adventure with the wolf took place, for he clearly knew a great deal about it, or at least about his version of it, a version that had distinctly

crystallized with the passage of time because, after all, some twenty years had passed, but for Alfredo it was as if the whole thing happened only yesterday since back then it was the only topic of conversation, and eventually he even boasted of seeing the wolf—yes, I saw it, the wolf, he repeated—the only trouble being that they wanted to see the actual place because Felix was away, Felix? yes Felix, the gamekeeper next door, and he was about to embark on further details of the hunt when a rusty old car screamed to a halt in front of them, as he told the barman at the Sparschwein, and Alfred ran out into the road, leaned in at the window of the car and spent some time talking to the driver before the car drew off again with Alfredo pointing after the car, saying Felix, that's Felix, but he can't see to you now because he's been told his grandfather has taken sick and is poorly, so he's going to see him in Herreuela to take him to the hospital, but he has promised to meet you tomorrow at ten in the morning at the entrance to the estate, the interpreter checking, at ten you say? and yes, Felix is bound to be here, Alfredo replied, you just make sure you're here then, and that was how they parted, he explained to the barman,

though it was only about two in the afternoon, which meant, said the interpreter, that they had plenty of time to meet someone else who might be interesting, and she told them that the Badajoz center had located a number of people who specialized in the story of wolves in the Sierra, including one who—if Herr Professor fancied—could meet them at four in Albuquerque which isn't far, the driver remarked, so okay, he answered, by all means let's go to Albuquerque, and to Albuquerque they went to meet a warden—a warden?—*a warden,* the interpreter bellowed, bellowed at him that is, he said pointing to himself in the Sparschwein, because he didn't know what the interpreter was talking about, *him,* she replied a little impatiently, unable to disguise the fact that by the middle of this third day she was finding it a bit tiresome coping with a guest who understood so little and was constantly asking her to repeat things, but never mind, she curled her lip, *him,* the man we are going to meet, that's the point, he is a wildlife warden and is waiting for us in the restaurant in Albuquerque at four, she said, raising her voice still further in the hope that this might help though it was unnecessary by then because

47

he had caught up and had understood that, yes, there was this man they were going to meet in Albuquerque, a warden, someone, they say, who really knows the area, the interpreter continued, a man who really knows wolves, in fact wolves are his spe-ci-al-it-y, she said, stressing each syllable of the word so as to give it weight, repeating, he's familiar with wolves, to which he responded by asking, as if to check, he's familiar with wolves? though he did gesture to her to indicate that he knew what she meant, and that he did not re-peat her words because he hadn't understood but be-cause of the way the idea had been expressed, since, you know, the sound of a phrase like "he's familiar with wolves," he told the Hungarian barman, in such an atmosphere, straight after the meetings with Chan-clon, Alfredo and Félix, in the presence of the inter-preter and the silent driver, carried a particular charge, so he began to look forward to the meeting with a cer-tain raised expectation, a raised expectation without really knowing what, in the circumstances, a proper sense of raised expectation might be, because, he had to be honest about it, the thought hadn't really oc-curred to him till now, he confessed to the barman, he

48

had not felt, not in the least, that the story was coming to its climax, a climax that would explain to him why fate had cast him here, a climax that would tell him what he should be doing, which would somewhat simplify matters for him with the foundation, a climax about which he knew nothing and the nature of which he could not begin to guess, though Albuquerque had a faintly haunting quality, perched, as it was, on top of an enormous peak in the middle of the plain, the slopes of which peak they were now climbing and where they soon parked, in front of a hotel that they entered to make their way through to the almost deserted restaurant, the few people in there mostly at the bar rather than at the tables of the restaurant itself, so they decided to wait there, ordering coffee, a glass of water and a beer, the three of them quietly sipping at their drinks and the interpreter attempting to start a conversation though no one felt much like talking; so they sat in silence for a while and thoughts began to run through his head, but, he had to confess, that by thoughts he didn't really mean what we usually mean by the term, more a condition of concentration, of concentrating his attention in a way that wasn't really

concentrated, and, even then, he was only using the term "concentration" to indicate a certain state in which he looked as if he were concentrating, when what was really going on was that he was entertaining a broken sequence of perfectly mundane thoughts, thoughts and images chasing each other round and round, one after the other, torturing him, which was how it was at home too he said, pointing through the window of the Sparschwein to the street, which was no different from what I was doing in Albuquerque, and so it went on for a short while, just one mundane thing after another, mere splinters of concentration, when, precisely at four, in stepped the warden, a tall, solid man of fifty-three or fifty-four, who came straight over to introduce himself as José Miguel, a man who, in full huntsman's gear, with steel framed glasses on his nose, his beard cut in a Newgate Fringe and an air of immediately impressive melancholy that he carried off with a certain military bearing, cut an altogether masculine figure, someone who, once he started speaking, clearly preferred short sentences, with longer or shorter silences between sentences, silences that carried as much significance as the sentences

themselves because he obviously gave careful consideration to all his utterances, which you could tell at first glance, he explained to the barman in the Sparschwein where it was going on for midday, the time when the first customers of the day tended to arrive, that is to say after the first wave of them who called in at early-morning opening time had disappeared for the morning as was the case with all the local bars around the top end of the Hauptstrasse, a mixed neighborhood, or rather a neighborhood that was preponderantly Turkish, but not entirely Turkish, the few bars serving alcohol at that time being crowded with Germans, Poles, Russians, Serbs, Romanians, Vietnamese and God knows who else, gulping down a cup of coffee or a glass of beer then setting straight off for wherever they were going, so that the bar was empty the rest of the morning, which might have been what appealed to this particular *Stammgast*, the barman muttered in Hungarian to the neat row of glasses ranged along the counter, because he was always here, whether he was wanted or not, though he, the barman, didn't mind him coming partly because all he did was drink two or three beers the whole day, and that meant

51

he, the barman, was not alone, because nothing was worse, damn it, than being alone and waiting—or so he occasionally complained when there was someone there to complain to—worse than hanging around by yourself behind the bar once you had done all the washing-up and rearranged the items on the counter for the hundredth time, not to mention tidying the storeroom at the back, so that everything was in place and there was nothing to do but wait, well, at such times it was good to have this German propping up the bar in the morning, and what was more his great bulk tended to frighten off those young Turkish kids who wandered in off the streets, who should have been at school or at work, and were up to no good, staring in, thinking that since neither the owner nor the barman was Turkish they could just smash the place up, but then they caught sight of this giant and took off, in other words, he put up with him even though he was neither Eastern European nor a decent looking chick, and when all was said and done this was a free country, and you can't say to people, you are not allowed in—so he sat there with his elbows on the counter listening, as it happened, to the story of how

the warden began by talking generally about the wolves near Albuquerque, refusing to answer any questions, saying he would give them a proper answer once they were in the place itself, smiling occasionally to assure them that he, and he pointed to himself, smiling, a little uncertainly at first but after a while in full confidence, that he, José Miguel, the warden, would show them everything they needed to see, and it was as though he had set out to make them feel that he was the only man, he pointed to himself, the only man who could help them explore the great story at proper depth—hold on, he didn't understand, the barman butted in, what great story he's talking about but was waved away as if to say, in a moment—so they all started by getting into the jeep and setting off to the spot where, and he had to yell over the noise of the jeep, with José Miguel occasionally looking at him, addressing him directly, the spot where the last wolf had perished—but perished? he queried, sharply, and gestured to the interpreter to clear the matter up—yes, the warden answered in his typically gruff way, that's where we're going, where the last wolf *perished*, but first we are going to see where the last *wolves* were

shot—what, wolves, plural? he twisted his whole body to face her, and what—even the Hungarian barman repeated, *the last wolves?*—what was the man talking about, he looked beseechingly at the interpreter in the back seat, and was eventually informed that the male wolf, the one they had gone to see in the glass case at Chanclon's, that wasn't really the last wolf, that incident happened, if he remembered right, in 1985, said the warden, in February, but after that, José Miguel emphasized in his staccato Spanish, there was a whole pack of wolves killed on the La Gegosa *finca*, to be precise between 1985 and 1988, and at that point they suddenly slowed and turned in through an ornate gatehouse—and then? asked the barman—and then he unlocked the chained gate, he answered, on which there was a brass plate saying La Gegosa, opening the gate wide so they could drive into the estate only stopping for a second to lock the gate again before they went on, and what they saw then, he dropped his voice, what they saw was not to be imagined, difficult even to speak about, because what they saw from the jeep as they were tossed from side to side—they had to hang on tight on account of the extraordinary speed

at which José Miguel drove them—this landscape opening up before them, was this *dehesa,* the grassy plain and, as far as the eye could see, all those masses of holly oak, so many it quite took their breath away, which was clearly what the warden expected, that he was waiting for them to be silent and to appreciate the nature of the sight opened before them, and that this might have been a kind of preliminary test they were supposed to face, a test to determine whether the visitors really understood where they were, a test, he said leaning on the counter, they must have passed, because José Miguel started speaking again, telling them about the place, about the creatures that lived here, from vultures through to deer, the jeep meanwhile rocking violently from side to side as José Miguel insisted on driving them at great speed over the rough, uneven terrain, there being no road, so even the interpreter had her hands full trying not to bang her head against the roof of the jeep, though she did bang it time and again, and the poor thing really had to bellow to explain what José Miguel was saying, and what José Miguel happened to be saying was that originally, when he was a young man working for a company

dealing with wildlife economy, his interest was in vultures and that the company entrusted him with anything to do with vultures since everyone knew he had a special relationship with vultures, that he understood their language, their needs and their emotions and that they, in turn, understood him, that he was completely unrivaled in his intimacy with vultures, that his feelings for them were of love and respect, that he regarded them as superior creatures—as what? he asked leaning back and the interpreter bellowed it out again loud as she could while trying to cover her head with both hands as they bumped to and fro in the speeding jeep, that they were su-pe-ri-or crea-tures—but José Miguel gave him a significant look through his steel framed glances, and continued, explaining that at that point a woman came into his life so he was faced with a choice between the vultures on the one hand and the woman on the other, and that he had chosen the woman in preference to the vultures, a decision he soon regretted, but that there was no going back to the vultures, which was how he found himself in a new field of study, here on this new estate, and he pointed through the jeep door, where there were orig-

inally a dozen wardens, though in recent years the number had been reduced to two, namely he himself and an older colleague, his boss, here in this protected area of a hundred thousand hectares, said José Miguel, where he started by giving names to the animals, calling one fox Ramiro and another Asunció for instance, and that there was a roebuck by the name of Jesús, and a fawn called Immaculada, and so forth, but then a bunch of rich people came down from Madrid, the kind of people who always succeed in getting a hunting license, and he had to drive them around, and these people, these people, repeated José Miguel, shot first Ramiro, then Asunció, then Immaculada, and finally Jesús too, and he found this very hard to take, which was when he stopped giving the animals names, because it was too painful to lose one or the other, at which point the warden gave him another significant look, he told the barman, his glasses flashing in the light so he could not see his eyes, and in any case he had to hold on tight so as not to be thrown around in the jeep which was approaching another gate, one of a series of gates, but by this time he himself lent a hand because this way they were saving time, and you know,

José Miguel said to him in thanking him for his help with the unlocking and locking of the gates, we do need to hurry if we want to see everything because it's getting on for half-past four which means we only have about another hour and a half or even less, so they got back into the car and continued speeding over the rough pathless ground of a place that, he remarked aloud, seemed to him like the garden of Eden, but José Miguel made no reply only nodded to indicate that he understood, and so they drove on for a while in silence until the jeep braked sharply to a stop and José Miguel got out, followed by the rest of them, and indicated first a tree, one oak among many, then pointed up the gentle slope to a faint barely discernible pathway, hardly more than a trail, telling them, in his usual staccato manner, that the tree was the one in whose branches sat the man who killed seven out of nine wolves between 1985 and 1988, it taking him a good three years to kill them, one after the other, alas, the wolves having for some unknown reason to follow this particular route, he said pointing to the path, this route, which was why the man found it so easy to murder them one after the other—murder? did he say

58

murder? he asked the interpreter, who understood immediately what was expected of her at such times, that is to check whether the warden did actually use that word in Spanish, and replied yes, it was here the wolves were mur-dered, she repeated in English — but after the death of the seventh, José Miguel went on, the man grew very frightened and lived for years in a perpetual state of fear, not just while perched in the tree, in other words on the nights he came here and took his place in the branches observing the wolves that came that way at particular times, but also when he went home in the morning, being frightened even at home, even at the pub, even when surrounded with friends, though the killing was something he was obliged to do on behalf of the gentry, he being employed precisely as a wolf-hunter, that's to say a *lobero*, the owner of the estate having hired him because he wanted nothing but the best, and this man, said José Miguel, really was the best, it was just that he was frightened and, as he said later, he wasn't most acutely frightened when the wolves were actually there, but before they arrived, when he saw nothing but the silent trail the wolves would follow to arrive there, for

naturally the pack was growing ever more wary with each death, but for some reason from time to time they continued using the trail, and the man was tough and patient, he persevered, and spent nearly every night for three years perched in those branches, and he had after all managed to shoot seven of them, but not the last two because after he had killed the last of the seven they no longer followed the trail, so even though the man carried on night after night for a very long time, each time taking up his position in the tree, he was eventually forced to give up because both the landowner and the owners of the neighboring *finca* lost patience with him, angry that despite being a *lobero* he was unable to finish off the last two, a fact that mattered to them not just because of the fear of the pack in the area but because the two remaining wolves occasionally attacked one or two of the older, possibly sick sheep or goats, and caused damage that led to the owners making complaints to the wolf-hunter who could do nothing, for the last two wolves had grown so wise to him that he never saw them again, nor for a long time did anyone else, the only evidence of them being their tracks, for the danger

had made them extraordinarily wary, this being a danger of which they were highly conscious, since only the two of them remained from the original pack and these two knew exactly what to expect if any man spotted them, so they constantly changed route and when, having ventured over to San Pedro, whose hills and general distance offered greater protection, they descended toward the flocks grazing below, they were even more careful, cleverer, wilier but courageous, and they never actually left, which surprised everyone who was aware of the story of the wolves, for people expected two such intelligent animals to move on elsewhere, but they stayed because, you know, said the warden as they set off in the jeep again, that's just the way wolves are, when they have made a territory theirs it remains theirs forever, it is their possession, and no matter if that territory extends over fifty hectares they still can't leave it, because that is their law, the law of the wolves, it's the way they think, it's their nature, and that was why they never left: they couldn't leave, not even though conscious of constant danger, it was impossible for them to leave that which was theirs, the territory whose borders they continued to mark, no,

that for them was quite impossible, and what's more, he, said José Miguel pointing at himself, he was utterly convinced that the law of the wolves comprised a good measure of pride, so it was safe to assume that it was, at least partly, pride that prevented them leaving, because wolves are very proud animals, proud, he declared almost spitting the word out then staring silently ahead, saying not a word, so that no one wanted to disturb him, for something had happened—he said to the Hungarian barman who had shut his eyes some time ago as he leaned on the counter ever more heavily, listening to the monotonous voice of the *Stammgast* in the empty bar—happened to José Miguel, as he could tell by the reaction of the interpreter, the man being completely under the spell of his own words, words that did not really come across in the English translation of course though they had clearly brought about a change him, conjuring something he didn't want to show to these strangers, which was why he stopped talking and stared stiffly ahead, his hands gripping the steering wheel as the jeep lurched across the uneven ground, throwing them this way and that, everyone holding on, waiting for José Miguel to con-

tinue, but it was a long time before he spoke again, and even then it was only to answer a question, not one he had put, but one asked by the interpreter who asked it in Spanish without translation so he couldn't tell what they were talking about, noticing only that the interpreter was vigorously nodding in agreement but still not translating as José Miguel spoke ever faster, until, once I had started giving her impatient looks, he said, she eventually explained that he was simply talking about wolves, how there was something marvelous about the characters of wolves, and the way she said this surprised me, he said, because her voice sounded quite different from before, it was distinctly trembling, and he wanted to ask her what had happened, what the warden had said that had so moved her, but did not ask just looked at her and then at José Miguel, and eventually she yelled out at the top of her voice that what José Miguel had been saying was that he was never disappointed in them and never would be, then José Miguel raised one hand from the wheel as a kind of warning that he had something else important to say—he even slowed the jeep a little though he was in any case crossing a small gully—saying, *el amor de los*

animales es el unico amor que el hombre puede cultiva sin cosechar el desengaño, or as the interpreter translated in English, "the love of animals is the one true love in which one is never disappointed," her voice still trembling — so what was that about, asked the barman behind the counter raising his sleepy head a little, to which he answered, well, that was to become clear later because, for lack of a translation, he himself didn't understand what it was about then — and to tell the truth he was cross with the interpreter because it seemed that, here in the jeep, a dialogue had sprung up between her and the warden and that he felt excluded from it, as indeed he was, but fortunately it was not for long because they soon arrived at the brow of a small hill where stood a deserted house where José Miguel applied the brakes and all three of them got out, José Miguel saying that he would like to sum up all he had said so far just so that it should be absolutely clear they the last wolf wasn't the one had been shot back in 1985 in the Cantillana de Vieja because the story of the last wolf was set here in the Cantillana La Gegos and began with the great wolf hunt to exterminate a whole pack with the help of a *lobero*, nine

wolves to be precise, but the *lobero* only killed seven, so the remaining two, a young female and an even younger male, succeeded in staying alive, though the locals didn't really understand how, since they had the services of a *lobero*, who, determined that he should not have cause for shame, not only spent each night in the tree but followed their tracks, paying close attention, noting the scent, and covered every inch of the whole estate without discovering them, his next step being to collaborate with local shepherds worried about their flocks because two wolves were still on the loose, to set up traps at every imaginable point, the traps being set near the end of 1988 and at the beginning of 1989, particularly savage traps, said the warden as he stood by the deserted building, and it was right here, here where we are standing, he pointed to the building, that they manufactured them, the whole apparatus no more than a piece of wire that worked on one simple ruthless principle, a noose at the end, the other tied very firmly to the bottom of the fence that separated different parts of the *finca*, wherever they noticed wolf trails, places here and there where the wolves had tunneled under looser fence posts and

slipped under them, explained José Miguel, so it was near these loose fences the local people set their traps under the direction of the *lobero*, and these were supposed to work, leaving the previous tunnels open, allowing the wolves through just far enough for their heads to be caught in the nooses that would, of course, grow ever tighter the more they struggled, and would eventually strangle them, but, Miguel's steel-rimmed glasses twinkled in the light, it didn't quite work out like that, nothing worked, the wolves came to no harm, though people couldn't understand why, not for a long time at least, for how could they avoid the nooses, then eventually they realized it was because the wolves never returned to the tunnels they had dug before, that's to say where the traps were, but always dug new ones, and indeed, said the warden, the wolves seemed to come and go as they pleased from one *finca* to another, moving at liberty between the individually fenced-off parts of each *finca,* those intended to separate the various animals, though since winters were relatively mild, they caused no great harm, and only rarely raided the flocks, and even those they took away were certain to be the older or sicker creatures who

were easier to catch, because that was how wolves are, but pretty soon people grew suspicious and looked for other reasons, said José Miguel raising his voice as he stood before the deserted house, the suggestion being that someone was helping them, for it was the only way they could explain how the wolves had succeeded in eluding them, because they had gone to all those extraordinary lengths to catch them but the wolves escaped every time; and some people were saying that there was something supernatural about the intelligence of these animals, that they blamed demons and even muttered something about ghosts, though the majority were more pragmatic in suspecting human agency and looked to discover who was helping the wolves, because, thought this majority, it couldn't be an accident that the traps were not working and, sure enough, when they examined the traps they found they had been loosened to the extent that if a wolf wanted to cross at one of its old crossings it could do so because the noose failed to tighten round its neck, the momentum of the creature dragging the wire away from the post so that a piece of it was left dragging behind for a while but the animal would keep shaking

67

its head until it had shaken it off, because there was no other way, they said with ever greater frequency, but that someone was behind this, and yet the idea seemed incredible because, surely, no one but an utter idiot would want to help the wolves, for man and wolf had been enemies for centuries, for thousands of years, and in any case, here they were now, they were a good few months into 1989 and the two wolves were still at liberty, so the shepherds went on looking for the man sabotaging their traps and eventually got themselves into such a state that they fired the *lobero*, but then noticed that the saboteur had moved on to other sites and was using different methods, that the earth by the fences had been disturbed just enough to allow one wolf at a time passage and they were sure this was not the animals' doing, nor some accident, but human work, the work of a dyed-in-the-wool villain, and so another bout of feverish activity began, trying to track the man down, but it ended almost as soon as it had started because at the end of 1989 it was reported to one of the wardens responsible for the estate, that warden being himself, José Miguel, that a wolf had been run over in a place near Caceres on the road to Bada-

joz, not far from the entrance to the *finca* called Cantillana Llomas de Grinaldo, at a point between the
thirtieth and thirty-first mile post, and that this was
one of the pair, the female; this was reported to him,
and being familiar with their movements, their behavior, their walks, even their faces, right from the very
beginning, in other words knowing them very well, he
was sure the report was right, and all this happened,
said José Miguel, because … but he did not continue
and much to their surprise simply got back behind the
wheel of the jeep and turned on the ignition but left
the engine off, so they followed him and sat down in
their places and waited, but José Miguel said nothing
for a long while, just looked out through the windshield, and eventually he turned the key and the engine started but they did not move off right away, instead he spoke again and said it was all because the
wolf was pregnant at which point the interpreter in the
back seat dissolved in tears and José Miguel continued
speaking piling one sentence on top of another, one
Spanish sentence running into the next, the interpreter so full of tears that she couldn't even speak let
alone translate, at which point he, he pointed to

69

himself in the Sparschwein, suddenly felt anything but empathy, rather rage, because he couldn't understand why he was being left to his own devices at the most exciting moment of the story, for the narrative having been broken in this way it seemed there was no need for him in this jeep, that he was redundant, because his heart was not broken the way the interpreter's clearly was, and all this made him utterly furious, furious with her, though he still didn't know why, couldn't know why, because he didn't think of himself as someone who could look on another human being in tears without feeling part of the grief, not just *not* feeling part of it in this case, he said, but feeling something quite perfectly vicious, and he was waiting only just in control of himself, and it was plain to see that the warden was in no better condition than the interpreter, that he made not the slightest effort to hide how affected he had been by his own story, that is to say by the memory, as José Miguel eventually continued—as he understood through the interpreter, and now José Miguel was looking at him directly, staring at him with a startled intensity as if the whole thing had happened just now—the memory, he repeated, for he could re-

member it clearly, could see that young she-wolf as clear as if it were yesterday, her guts spilled, her crushed belly with the dead cub inside it, could see it even now and always would see it, and he was sure that the wolf had been hit because, and only because, she was pregnant, because her belly was already too large and so *she could not run* across the road fast enough to escape the accident prepared for her, probably an accident, but possibly intended by the driver-murderer, and when he thought about this he simply stood there, rooted to the spot, in the middle of the road with the dead animal beside him while passing cars sounded their horns at him and swerved around him, though he seemed to hear them as if at a great distance, because he was helpless standing there, and if his colleague, the older warden, hadn't arrived he might have stayed there with the dead animal, and he too might have been run over, that being his condition when his older colleague yanked him to the roadside, first him and then the wolf, the colleague having to do this all by himself because he himself was quite incapable of movement and hardly knew what he was doing, simply doing what he was told, but together

71

eventually they dragged the wolf into the roadside ditch and immediately buried her too, that was where she was buried, even today he could point to the place, though you, he said, looking into his eyes again as he started the jeep, would find nothing but bones there now of course, that is if you found anything at all, but let's drop the subject, he said, clearing his throat and putting his foot down on the gas, so that they were speeding once more and he fell silent again for a long time simply gazing through the windshield at the scene in front of him, while the interpreter apologized, three times, three times, because she felt she had lost control of herself on account of all she had heard, and she really didn't know, or so she bellowed over the noise of the jeep, what had come over her, but the warden's story had affected her so much, so much ... but he waved to indicate that it was all right, to say, never mind, he explained to the barman having failed to notice that the man had long stopped listening and had nodded off, that he was fast asleep, no doubt dreaming, a fact he had failed to notice because he had turned away from him to gaze through the window at the street—but now he felt the same anxiety

he had felt then, back at the scene he had been describing, and was horrified to note that his feeling of anxiety was more pressing, more intense, more insistent, than the sense of emptiness that constituted his very being, the calm, perfectly relaxed sense of emptiness he was used to, and this anxiety, he said aloud, pointing at himself again, the anxiety he first felt in the jeep after hearing José Miguel's story, but most powerfully only on the way back as the sky grew dark when José Miguel told him how the young male wolf vanished, his tracks leading them to think he had migrated toward the Portuguese border and however much, he said staring into the desert of the Hauptstrasse, however much he wanted José Miguel's story to be over at this point, that is with the line that the young male wolf vanished over the Portuguese border, *just like that*, the story did not end there because they made a considerable detour to view the stretch between the thirtieth and thirty-first mile post on the Badajoz road, then retraced their route, without any explanation, to La Gegosa to inspect a spot beside a small pond, before finally returning to Albuquerque, reaching the door of the hotel where they had first met

at four o'clock at which point José Miguel summoned
up a single, dry, factual, tragic sentence, about how
they did not know for a while what had happened to
the remaining wolf, everyone having believed that it
had vanished somewhere in Portugal, but then one
day in 1993 they discovered it had not gone anywhere,
that there was no Portugal waiting for it, because one
early dawn a shepherd, a certain Alexandro, rang him
to come at once because he had shot a wolf by a pond
on the *finca*, and once there it was not difficult to confirm that this was what had been the young male wolf,
who, it seemed, had never abandoned its territory but
had remained within the Cantillana la Gegosa where,
despite years of success, it could not avoid its fate, and
so I am obliged to tell you, said the warden, that the
man you are looking for is Alexandro, the man who
shot him, and so José Miguel took his leave of the interpreter and of the driver who had just arrived to
fetch them, but first he asked me, he said, to accompany him to the jeep because he had something else
to say, directly to me, something just between the two
of us, saying he would try to do so in English faintly
smiling as he said it, and so they went over to the jeep

where José Miguel cleared his throat, looked straight in his eyes and told him, in broken English, that he had something he wanted to confess—but hey, wake up, he shouted turning round to face the barman at the counter, who jerked his head up, blinking in confusion, wakey-wakey! I am just about to tell you what it was the warden wanted to tell me back at his jeep, yeah, so what was it, grumbled the Hungarian barman and rubbed his eyes—well, it was precisely what I expected, he said, so I told him not to tell me, we simply embraced, and that was how I left him, and this is how he brought on the sense of anxiety that I still suffer from to this very day—oh right, anxiety, grinned the barman, yawning and stretching his back still sitting down, muttering to himself in Hungarian, go on then, go tell your story, you last of the wolves, go on, I'm listening—and yes, he replied, turning to face the window, but did not continue, saying nothing more for how could he explain that though he had returned to the place he had left in order to make a brief visit to Extremadura, what remained for him was a life without thought, in other words the deathly wasteland of the Sparschwein, this cold, empty, hollow square, and

the fact that he had not earned this or that amount of Euros for doing as asked but had instead locked Extremadura in the depths of his own cold, empty, hollow heart, and that ever since then, day after day, he had been rewriting the end of José Miguel's story in his head, and that that's exactly where he was now, at the end.

TRANSLATED BY GEORGE SZIRTES